Faye & the Music Fairies

The Clef Crystal

Paul Govier-Simpson

Text Copyright ©2015 Lyssa-Jade Simpson

The right of Paul Govier-Simpson to be identified as the author of this work has been asserted by her daughter, Lyssa-Jade Simpson.

All rights reserved.

ISBN:9798327150638

This book is sold subject to the condition that it shall not, by way of trade or otherwise, be lent, hired out or otherwise circulated in any form of binding or cover other than that in which it is published.

No part of this publication may be reproduced, stored in a retrieval system, transmitted in any form of means (electronic, mechanical, photocopying, recording or otherwise) without the written permission of Lyssa-Jade Simpson, Copyright holder.

Illustrations Copyright ©2021 Joelle Henry

OTHER BOOKS IN THE FAYE & THE MUSIC FAIRIES SERIES

1 The Clef Crystal

2 Scales

3 Dee Sharp

4 Woodwind

5 Crescendo

6 Tutti

ACKNOWLEDGEMENTS

Thank you to Lynda, Hannah, Chloe, Millie, Julia (and anyone else I have forgotten!) for sitting and listening to mum read you excerpts of her books, and giving her the reactions and feedback that she needed to hear. you all played a big part in shaping the characters.

Thank you to the wonderful staff at Grants Cafe in Okehampton for letting mum sit at table 11 every Monday for months on end supplying her with endless cups of coffee to enable her to write these books. "Hufflepuff" was very grateful!

Thank you to the wonderful Jo, (who has created the beautiful illustrations) for helping me bring mum's creation to life - I could not have asked for anyone better or more talented!

Thank you to Kelly for doing all the proofreading, and fitting it in between your busy schedule!

Finally, a big thank you to my sisters, Layla and Starla, who helped me de-code mum's hieroglyphic handwriting whilst I was typing up these books - I couldn't have done it without you!

NOTE FROM THE AUTHOR'S DAUGHTER

After promising mum that I would get these books published, I didn't realize what a tough challenge it would be! All 6 books were hand written in A5 notebooks, with editing marks throughout that coincided with notes in different notepads altogether.

It has taken me nearly a year to type up the first two, with book 1 being the only one that has been edited and ready to be published, but as ever, I will persevere so that I can bring mum's magical stories to you.

Mum – I hope this is how you wanted your books to be, trying to delve into your brain and asking myself "what would mum have wanted?" or "what would mum have done/said?" These have been constant questions on my mind during this crazy process!

I hope you are flying high and happy, forever our beautiful butterfly.

Love you always, Mum.

Lyssa -x-

CHAPTER 1

"Bye, Faye! See you at school!"

"Bye, Faye! Thanks for asking us!"

"Bye!" called Faye, watching the twins, Jordan and James, and her best friend, Peri, running through the rain to Peri's mum's car.

"Happy birthday, again!" yelled Peri as she climbed in.

Faye watched until the silver Fiesta disappeared round the corner, then she shut the front door. It had been a brilliant day; ice skating with Mum and Peri in the morning and then six friends (including Peri) over in the afternoon for computer games, and burgers and chips. Now she was eight. It felt good. So much better than seven!

"Had a nice day, love?" her mum asked.

"Brilliant! Thanks, Mum." Faye gave her a hug. It was only the two of them, and Faye knew her mum found it hard to provide treats.

"Now, do you want anything else to eat?"

"No thanks, I'm stuffed with burgers and birthday cake!"

Mum chuckled, shaking her head. "Back to proper food tomorrow."

Faye laughed. "I know! Do you mind if I go and look at all my presents up in my room now, Mum?"

"Of course not, love. I've got all this lot to clear up anyway; off you go!"

"No, I'll help you first." Faye knew her mum would be getting ready to do the night shift at the local twenty-four-hour supermarket soon, and Mrs Thomas from next door would be coming in to 'baby sit'.

"But it's your birthday, Faye…" began Mum, shaking her head.

"Yes," agreed Faye, "and if we both do it, you'll have time to sit and talk to me before you leave."

Mum smiled. "You are a thoughtful girl, come on then."

Faye's mum fetched a tray and together they cleared the table, taking everything into the small kitchen. Mum washed up while Faye dried and put everything away.

"There, all done!" said Mum. "Now we can have a good look at all your presents – ooh, I nearly forgot!" She went to reach up on top of the fridge. "This arrived for you a couple of days ago, so I hid it."

"Thanks, Mum." Faye took the envelope from her; she knew who it was from at once. 'Miss Faye Martin' was written in big, swirly, loopy writing. "Great Aunt Laura!" she said to Mum.

"Yes, but there's no present, which is unusual; maybe she's finally running out of money!

"Maybe," echoed Faye, thoughtfully. Great Aunt Laura was her dad's aunt and after he'd died, she'd been very good to Faye and her mum: 'settling bills' Mum had called it. They were grateful, of course, but Faye knew her mum hated asking Great Aunt Laura for money and never did so if she could possibly help it.

"Come on, open it up!" Mum broke into Faye's thoughts.

"Sorry." Faye opened the posh, lilac envelope and pulled out a card with flowers, birds and butterflies on the front.

'That would be lovely…if I was forty!' thought Faye, though she didn't say it aloud as she knew her mum would tell her off.

Faye went to open the card, when something slid out of it and fell on the floor.

"What's that?" said Mum, bending to pick it up. She glanced at it, then paused, read it again and silently handed it to Faye.

Faye looked at the stiff, white card with the copperplate writing which said: 'Miss Faye Martin, on the occasion of her eighth birthday, has been given a course of piano lessons, to begin on Friday next. Miss Hummingstone will be with you at 5pm sharp.

Many happy returns, your affectionate aunt, Laura Langley.'

"Piano lessons?!" Faye stared blankly at her mum, who replied with a slight frown.

"I know, love. But I did wonder if this might happen one day."

"Why?" queried Faye.

"Come and sit down." Mum led the way back into their cosy front room and patted the sofa. Faye sat next to her mum.

"Listen, Faye, you were so young when Dad died that you probably don't remember a lot about him."

This was true – Faye could just about recall a tall figure with floppy, brown hair who threw her up high, laughing as he caught her again, but truthfully, without the photo Mum kept on top of his old piano in the corner, Faye would have found it hard to remember his face, so she shook her head.

Mum went on, "Your Great Aunt Laura was a famous pianist in her day, but she gave it all up to marry your Great Uncle Edgar. They never had any children and when her husband died, just before your dad was born, she took a keen interest in him and had him playing the piano almost as soon as he could walk! Your dad played to please her, but wasn't really very interested or, to be honest, very good at it!" Mum laughed softly, glancing at the old piano, fondly. "I remember him sitting there, plonking away, trying to copy some song he'd heard on the radio…and he never got it right!"

Faye thought back hard but couldn't remember ever hearing her dad play.

"Oh, this was before you were born." Mum said, as if guessing Faye's thoughts. "Once we had you, he was much more interested in playing with you than playing the piano…Oh dear, I've gone completely off what I was going to say!" Mum sighed.

"The point is, Faye, Great Aunt Laura was always disappointed that no one else in the family had inherited her talent. When you were born, she said, 'Well, let's wait and see what this little one becomes.' So, you see, I guess she feels now is the time to discover if you're any good."

"But I won't be!" said Faye, horrified. "You know I'm rubbish at learning new things – look at swimming!" Swimming was a very sore point between Faye and her mum; she'd gone swimming with the school, and, during the whole course, she'd had to be fished out of the water by the lifeguard no less than five times! Faye had point-blank refused to learn to swim EVER, after that.

"You don't know that you'll be rubbish," argued Mum. "You might be surprised at how good you could be, if you'd only give yourself a chance, love."

They were interrupted by a knock at the front door.

"That'll be Mrs Thomas, and I'm not ready! Quick, let her in, will you?"

Mum dived upstairs as Faye went to open the front door.

"Hello, Mrs Thomas."

"Hello, Faye. Happy birthday!" said Mrs Thomas, handing her a small bag.

Faye smiled as she accepted the gift. "Thank you. Please come in."

The little Welsh lady sailed into the front room and sat herself down on the sofa with a sigh; there was quite a lot of Mrs Thomas, so sitting down and getting up were always accompanied by sighs. Faye peeked inside the bag and, sure enough, there was a bar of her favourite chocolate and a birthday card. Mrs Thomas had done this on Faye's birthday ever since she started coming in on those evenings when Mum had to work, five years ago.

"Sorry, Mrs Thomas!" Faye's mum dashed in. "I'm late!" She glanced at Faye. "What's that you've got, chocolate? Did you say thank you? Don't eat it all tonight. Brush your teeth after. Don't stay up too late, oh and…happy birthday, love!"

She kissed Faye on the cheek. "Thanks, Mrs Thomas!" This came as Mum flew out the front door.

"Your poor mum works too hard," said Mrs Thomas, shaking her head.

"Thank you for the card and chocolate, Mrs Thomas," said Faye, setting them down on the table.

"That's alright, my dear. Now, you go and do whatever it is you young folk find to do while I watch my programme, and then we'll have a hot chocolate."

"Okay!" Faye picked up the bar of chocolate and Great Aunt Laura's card from the coffee table. "I'll be up in my room, then."

Mrs Thomas had already switched on the TV and merely waved a hand in Faye's direction to show that she had heard.

Faye shot upstairs into her room and shut the door with a sigh of relief; finally, she could examine all her presents at leisure! There they were, piled up on the bed. Mum had bought her the new computer game she really wanted, which Faye knew had cost more than her mum could afford. She wondered what Mum had gone without to pay for it, but that was her mum all over. Faye hugged the game to her chest, grateful for such a lovely surprise. The twins had got her a Digi Bird that talked and a bracelet-making kit; Chloe Harris, who, at the moment, was being nice to Faye (although that could change from week to week), had given her a pink T-shirt with a cat on it, and Millie, who was very artistic, had made her a notice board with a border of leaves, all cut out of different fabrics and glued in layers on top of each other. The effect was very pretty, and Faye really liked it. Lucy, her second-best friend, had given her a voucher for games or DVDs, and Peri had bought her the lockable diary which Faye had wanted for ages! It was pink with 'gemstones' decorating the borders all around the front; Faye stroked it admiringly. She loved writing. When they had to write essays at school, she was always the last to put down her pen, and now she could write whatever she liked in her diary and keep it – just to read for herself! She took Mrs Thomas's card out of the bag and read it: 'Happy Birthday Faye, lots of love from Mrs Thomas'. Faye smiled as she broke off a piece of chocolate and popped it into her mouth. As she put her diary back on top of the pile of presents, she saw the card from Great Aunt Laura. She picked it up and the voucher inside fell out. "Piano lessons!" she said to herself, as she went to put her cards up on her bookshelf with all the others. "Why me?"

CHAPTER 2

It was Friday. It was ten to five. Faye sat on the sofa, fidgeting nervously. She hated meeting people for the first time; it made her feel sick with nerves, she was so sure they wouldn't like her!

Mum had pointed out that most people did, in fact, like her, but it didn't make Faye feel any better the next time it happened. Bang on five o'clock there was a knock on the door. Faye jumped!

"That'll be Miss Hummingstone," called Mum from the kitchen.

"Let her in, Faye, will you?"

Faye reluctantly went to the front door and opened it.

"Hello, are you Faye?" said a brisk but friendly voice.

Faye risked a glance upwards for a second and caught a glimpse of a wide, pleasant face, framed by dark, curly brown hair.

"Yes, come in." Faye tried to sound welcoming but heard herself coming across as sulky.

"I'm Miss Hummingstone," the voice went on. "Is your mum here?"

"Just coming," called Mum, bustling out of the kitchen. "Would you like a drink?"

"No, thank you, I just wanted to introduce myself; I'm Sarah Hummingstone."

"Pleased to meet you," said Mum, shaking her hand while Faye stood there awkwardly.

"Now," Miss Hummingstone smiled at Faye, "we need to get started, as I have other students to teach tonight."

"Here we are, then." Mum indicated the piano, where she'd pulled up a chair next to the old piano stool.

"Thank you," said Miss Hummingstone. "Now, Faye, if you'll sit on the stool…"

There then followed the longest half-hour of Faye's short life.

Miss Hummingstone was very kind and kept explaining things to her.

"Each finger is given a number, and then the numbers are written over the notes of each exercise, so you play them correctly."

Faye nodded, not really understanding.

"So, Faye – the thumb is 1, forefinger 2, middle finger 3, ring finger 4 and pinkie 5. Now, this is middle C."

Miss Hummingstone pointed to a white note. "We use letters of the alphabet to name the notes on the piano, so we can identify them." On and on it went, Miss Hummingstone explaining and Faye thinking: "I won't be any good at this; I don't understand!"

"Now, let's see how many other Cs you can find."

Faye looked at the black and white keys stretching out before her…'Not a clue!' she thought. Miss Hummingstone pointed out the shape of the surrounding notes. "Look at this shape, Faye; can you see it again further up?" After a lot of looking, Faye found another C. "This one?" she asked.

"Very good, Faye; that's right!"

By the end of the lesson (and with a lot of help from Miss Hummingstone) Faye had found, and played, all the Cs on the piano. "That'll do for today," said Miss Hummingstone.

Faye couldn't help heaving a sigh of relief.

"Can I have a word with your mum before I leave?"

As if by magic, Mum appeared from the kitchen.

"You'll need to have your piano tuned, Mrs Martin, if Faye is to learn properly."

"Alright…er…thank you." Mum sounded worried; Faye guessed it would be expensive.

"I'm leaving you with a couple of simple exercises to practice for next week, Faye," said Miss Hummingstone, propping a small book up on the music stand of the piano. "You'll need to do them every day…and I'll know if you haven't!"

She looked at Faye. "Practice makes perfect. Thank you, Mrs Martin, I'll see myself out."

She was gone before Faye or her mum could think of anything else to say. "Well…" began Mum, but just then the doorbell rang. "She must have forgotten something." Mum went to open the door, and then Faye heard her "Oh!" of surprise.

Faye was amazed when who should walk in but Great Aunt Laura!

"Hello!" Faye said in astonishment; she'd only ever seen her great aunt at her house. Three times a year, Faye and her mum took a train journey to the big, old, draughty house where Great Aunt Laura lived – she'd never been to their tiny maisonette before. "Are…are you staying the night, Aunt Laura?" stammered Faye's mum, wondering, Faye thought, where they could put her.

"No, no, Jenny, dear, I'm staying at a hotel for a couple of nights, nearby. I just thought I'd call in to see how Faye's first piano lesson went..." She raised an enquiring eyebrow at Faye, who stuttered: "Well...um...yes, it was...I had to find a lot of middle Cs" she ended in a rush.

"There is only one middle C," Great Aunt Laura replied. "I think you mean you had to find all the other Cs."

"Yes, that's right!" Faye was relieved to see she'd understood.

"And did you?"

"Did I what?"

"Find all the other Cs!"

Faye gulped. "Yes, but Miss Hummingstone had to explain a few times what the notes next to them looked like."

"I see." Great Aunt Laura didn't sound impressed. "Well, there's time to improve. The other reason I came was to give you this..." She held out a small, flat package to Faye.

Faye looked at her mum doubtfully. "But, I...I thought the piano lessons were my birthday present?"

"They are," replied her aunt. "This is something extra – it only came to light yesterday."

Faye took the package and gave a small gasp; it was a lot heavier than it looked! She sat on the floor and opened the package on her lap. Inside the tissue paper which covered it was a long, flat box. Faye opened it. As she saw what was inside, she quickly tried to make her face go into a happy and excited expression, but heard her mum having exactly the same reaction for, inside the box, lay a heavy, Victorian-looking necklace! It was made of silver and had a blue enamel bit at the bottom; the top of the pendant looked a bit like an 8 which had gone a bit 'squonky', with a curly piece in the middle and at the bottom of the silver section. However, in the middle curl sat the sparkliest stone that Faye had ever seen! The whole thing was suspended from a short, heavy, silver chain, and it looked like something Queen Victoria might have worn! Faye looked at her mum, stunned.

"Er... Aunt Laura, this is very generous..." began Faye's mum, hesitantly, "but... er...Faye is only eight!"

"I know how old she is," snapped Great Aunt Laura. "This is a family heirloom; it has been handed down from generation to generation. It should have gone to dear Kieran of course" (dear Kieran was Faye's dad) "but it's been missing for the last thirty years. One of the removal men found it down the back of my old chest of drawers – I have no idea how it got there!"

"Oh, an heirloom?" Mum appeared to be relieved. "So, it's to keep for when Faye's older?"

"No," insisted the old lady, "she's to wear it now. Whenever she comes to see me and whenever she practises the piano!" Faye looked helplessly at her.

"Well, that's all I came for." Great Aunt Laura got up. "I have a cab waiting outside. Happy birthday for last week, Faye."

She turned to Faye's mum and pushed an envelope into her hand. "For emergencies, Jenny dear." She turned and walked to the front door, when she looked back at Faye. "By the way, the piano tuner will be here in two weeks' time. Meanwhile, practice!" and she was gone.

"She's barking!" Faye turned to her mum and stopped; Mum was crying! "Mum…what's wrong?" Faye ran over to her. Mum shook her head, holding up the open envelope Aunt Laura had given her. Faye gasped as she saw it was stuffed with money! "So generous," Faye's mum sobbed. "I can pay the gas and the electric now." Faye made her mum sit on the sofa.

Mum dried her eyes and tried to smile at Faye. "You mustn't call her 'barking', Faye; it's not very kind. She's not mad, just a little bit eccentric, you know, she just sees things in a different light, that's all."

"But Mum, why does she want me to wear a huge old necklace when I'm practising the piano – it doesn't even make sense!"

"I know, dear, but we couldn't survive without her help, so just do it to please her, will you? Promise?" Faye promised at once. Her mum only ever asked for her promise on really important things like being careful crossing the road and 'stranger danger'. So, if mum thought it was that important, she'd do it – no questions asked.

As Faye sat on her bed later that evening she stared at the necklace. It was sort of pretty, she supposed, or would have been if it wasn't so heavy!

She tried it on for size and looked in the mirror on her wardrobe door.

Was it a trick of the light, or was the stone in the middle glowing? Faye moved a bit nearer the mirror; it was glowing! And now Faye could hear a very faint note, as if someone was singing out in the street.

Faye dashed to the window and looked out – no one there. She took off the necklace and flung it on the bed.

Faye reached out a hesitant finger and touched the stone – nothing! No glow, no note! She quickly put the necklace back in its box and put the box away in her chest of drawers.

Faye got ready for bed, and as she heard Mum calling "Bye!" and Mrs Thomas call "Hello" as they passed each other at the front door, Faye started to head downstairs for her weekly game of Scrabble with Mrs Thomas when a thought struck her. "Miss Hummingstone only told us today that we had to get the piano tuned, but Great Aunt Laura had already organised it before we knew!" This whole piano thing was getting more of a mystery by the minute!

CHAPTER 3

Over the next two weeks, Faye did her best to follow Miss Hummingstone's instructions – she learned to name all of the notes on the piano, but she'd only played the white ones so far! The black notes were, apparently 'sharps' and 'flats', and Faye was told that she would play them eventually, but practising was something she was beginning to hate! It was the last thing Miss Hummingstone said as she left and the first thing Aunt Laura asked about when she rang Faye's mum (which was every Friday now, after Faye's lesson)

Then there was Mum herself. "Have you done your practice, Faye?" Mum would call up the stairs after school each day.

"Just coming," Faye would call back, and, with a sigh, go down into the front room to do it.

If it hadn't been for Aunt Laura, and Mum not wanting to offend her, Faye would have given it up on the spot. She was just thinking this as she sat down at the piano, when there was a knock at the door.

"Answer it, love, will you?" called Mum from the kitchen.

"Okay." Faye ran to the front door and opened it. There, much to her surprise, was a large dog!

"Hello!" Faye said, reaching out to pet him. Jordan and James had a large, black, fluffy dog, so she was quite used to them.

Then she noticed that the dog, a friendly-looking honey-coloured Labrador, was wearing a strange sort of harness around his chest, with a stiff handle attached to it.

She looked along the handle and saw it was being held by an old man with dark glasses on.

"Mum," Faye called, knowing she wasn't supposed to let people she didn't know into the house; Mum was very strict on that!

Mum came out, drying her hands. "Hello, can I help you?"

"Hello," the old man said, putting a card out for Mum to take. "I hope I'm at the right address. I've come to tune your piano!"

Mum took the card and read it out. 'A. Tonal – Piano Tuner.' But…but that's tomorrow!" cried Mum – "On the 14th – I have it marked on the calendar!"

"Today is the 14th." Mr Tonal smiled gently.

"No…is it?" Mum was amazed. "I thought…oh I'm so sorry, please come in!"

"Is it alright if Tanzy comes too? She's my eyes, you see."

"Of course." Mum walked into the front room, talking all the time. "If you'll just follow me in here, that's right. Now the piano is just to your right. It's an upright."

Faye shut the front door and followed the old man in. What was wrong with her mum? Why was she telling the man where the piano was – he could see it right there in front of him!

"Can I get you anything?" Mum asked.

"A cup of tea would be lovely," Mr Tonal replied. "And where should I put my coat?"

"You saw the coat stand in the hallway!" Faye blurted out before she could stop herself.

"Faye!" Mum only ever used that tone of voice when Faye was in big trouble!

"It's alright, Mrs Martin, she's young – why should she know?" He turned towards Faye. "I'm blind, you see," he said cheerfully. "That's why I need Tanzy here." He patted the dog's head. "She sees for me, stops me getting run over or falling down steps."

"Oh, sorry!" Faye felt terrible – she ought to have realised when she saw the dog-harness!

"That's alright." Mr Tonal smiled.

"Now, would you like to see how a piano is tuned?"

"Oh yes please. Can I, Mum?"

"As long as you don't get in Mr Tonal's way," said Mum, looking sternly at her.

"She won't." Mr Tonal took his coat off and Faye's mum took it from him.

"I'll see about that tea for you." She went into the hallway and hung up his coat, before returning to the kitchen.

"Now, you can be my helper. Can you see a little hammer and a spanner in my case?"

Faye opened it and looked. "Yes," she said.

"Please can you get them out for me and put them on the piano stool?" Faye did so.

"How did you know there's a piano stool?" Faye asked.

"Well, for one thing, most pianos have a piano stool, and secondly," he smiled at her. "I felt it when I put the case down just now!"

"Of course!" Faye felt a bit stupid.

"Don't worry so," Mr Tonal said as he opened up the top of the piano and bent down to remove the panel at the front, where the pedals were.

"You're not being a nuisance, are you, Faye?" Mum said as she came in with the tea.

"No, she isn't – she's being helpful," replied Mr Tonal, turning to face Faye's mum.

"I'll just put your tea on the small table, to your left."

"Thank you, Mrs Martin."

With a 'behave yourself' sort of look at Faye, Mum went back into the kitchen.

Faye sat down next to Tanzy, who had flopped down on the floor as soon as Mr Tonal had let go of her handle, and stroked the dog gently.

"She likes you," Mr Tonal said, surprising her. "Tanzy is a very good judge of character – she's never wrong about people."

"I like her, too!" Faye was more relaxed around animals than people, sometimes.

After a pause, Mr Tonal said, "So…Faye, is it? How long have you been having piano lessons?"

"Three weeks." Faye frowned. "And I'm rubbish at it!"

"Really?" Mr Tonal sounded surprised. "Why did you ask to learn, then?"

"I didn't!" Suddenly the unfairness of the whole situation made Faye want to scream! "My great aunt is making me have piano lessons, because she was a great pianist, and my dad's dead so she's given me this stupid heavy necklace!" Faye burst into tears – she knew she wasn't making any sense, but she was just miserable.

"A necklace, you say?" Mr Tonal replied in the calmest of voices, just as if she hadn't had a complete meltdown in front of him. "What sort of necklace?"

Faye sniffed, drew in a shuddering breath and said, "It's heavy, old-fashioned. It has a silver squiggly thing and a blue flicky thing on the bottom and the middle bit glows sometimes, or…it did once," she amended.

Mr Tonal dropped his hammer. "Could I see it, do you think, Faye?"

"See it?" Faye was puzzled.

"By that, of course, I mean feel it!" Mr Tonal smiled.

"I'll get it." Faye ran upstairs and came back with the long, flat box. She opened it in front of him and put the necklace into the piano tuner's hands. He felt it carefully, running his fingers over the shapes and round the curves. When he came to the stone in the middle, he let out a long sigh. "Aah…"

"What is it?" asked Faye.

"This is a very special necklace," Mr Tonal replied as he handed it back to her. "In fact, I shouldn't be at all surprised if it didn't turn out to be magic."

"Magic?!" Faye was astonished. Grown-ups, as a rule, didn't believe in magic. "How does it work?"

"That, you'll have to discover on your own," he said mysteriously.

Faye looked at the necklace in her hands as Mr Tonal continued to work. What would the necklace do? She wondered…maybe it would turn her into the best pianist ever! That would be some trick, she thought.

"There are no shortcuts to learning an instrument." Mr Tonal made her jump – how had he guessed what she was thinking? "You have to practice!" Faye groaned – how she hated that word! "It's the only way…" he continued gently. "Trust me, Faye. And now…" he suddenly played a loud fanfare on the keys, "you have a perfectly tuned piano to practice upon!"

Faye listened, completely entranced, as Mr Tonal went from playing a loud march, to a soft, beautiful, flowing tune, to a melody so sad she almost started to cry and finally to a song her Mum sang which was on the car CD!

"How do you do that?!" Faye cried, clapping her hands in delight as he finished the medley with a 'plinky-plonk'.

"When you can't see, your other senses get better, almost as if to make up for it. My particular gift is, once I've heard a tune a couple of times, I can play it. I feel where the notes come – I don't have to see them."

"That was wonderful!" Mum had come in unnoticed and was applauding too!

"Your piano is tuned, Mrs Martin." Mr Tonal stood up. Tanzy looked at him and got up also, positioning herself so that the harness handle fell easily into his hand.

"Er…how much do we owe you?" Mum said awkwardly, hoping she had enough, Faye guessed.

"All paid for." He smiled. "Mrs Langley settled with me on the day I met her when she booked me."

"You know Great-Aunt Laura?!" Faye said in amazement.

"Oh yes, we're old friends. Now, if I could just get my coat, Mrs Martin?"

"Yes, of course." Mum hurried into the hall to fetch it.

"Remember, Faye," Mr Tonal's voice was suddenly serious, "always wear the necklace when you practice!"

Faye was so surprised that she could think of nothing to say. How did he know? At that moment Mum returned with the coat, and two minutes later Tanzy had led Mr Tonal to the door and the two of them left with Mr Tonal's "Goodbye ladies" echoing in the doorway.

"Well," said Mum, shutting the door. "That's a relief! I thought it was going to be really expensive! Right, Faye – you have no excuses now. You have a lesson tomorrow and Miss Hummingstone wants that piece learned, remember!"

"But, Mum…" Faye started to moan, and then stopped as she looked at her mum's concerned face.

"I know, love. But please can't we just humour Aunt Laura on this – it's not a whole lot to ask in return for what she does for us, is it?"

"I suppose not," grumbled Faye, flopping onto the piano stool with a sigh.

"That's my girl." Mum smiled. "I'm going to make some little cakes as a reward, but I'll be listening!" Mum gave a little laugh as she returned to the kitchen.

Faye reached for her music book, but as she opened it, she remembered Mr Tonal's instructions. She reached for the necklace where she'd left it on the coffee table and, undoing the heavy clasp, put it round her neck and did it up.

'I feel really silly,' she thought, 'wearing some fancy necklace to play the piano!'

But she opened her book. She was to learn 'Twinkle, Twinkle Little Star'. As she began to play, Faye sighed. She kept getting the third note wrong. She could do the first 'twinkle', that was easy as it was the same note (middle C) placed twice, but the next note, the one that started the second 'twinkle', she just couldn't find! Sometimes it went too high, sometimes too low. She knew she was supposed to count on her fingers from the thumb – 1, 2, 3, 4, 5, - but she kept forgetting, so by the third note she'd forgotten which finger and which note it was!

After the fourth failed attempt Faye got cross! The necklace was heavy; she couldn't play it. Stupid necklace! Stupid piano!

She brought her hands crashing down on any notes her fingers could find.

Suddenly, her necklace started glowing! There was no mistaking it this time, and a high-pitched humming sounded from the centre of the silver symbol.

Faye swung round off the piano stool and lifted her necklace up to look at it, but found she was looking through it, at a little path of silver sparkles leading to a blue and silver archway! Faye lowered the necklace slowly and everything disappeared, so with trembling hands she raised the necklace, looked through it again and, even though she knew she would bang into the wall any minute, Faye stepped along the sparkle pathway until she reached the blue and silver arch, and then…

She went through it!

CHAPTER 4

Faye blinked hard and looked around her. She appeared to be in a little round meadow, wildflowers grew everywhere. She could name some of them. Buttercups and daisies, poppies and blue cornflowers – all making the grass look like an artist's palate. A ring of brightly coloured butterflies danced overhead; birds sang in the distance. Faye thought she had never seen such a beautiful place.

Suddenly, one of the flower heads started to move, then it began to giggle!

Faye spun round to her right to the place of the sound as…a figure stood up! It had bright blue hair, a slender figure, and…wings!

"You're…you're a fairy!" gasped Faye.

"Yes, I am," said the fairy. "A music fairy, to be precise."

"A music fairy?" murmured Faye, not understanding at all. "Where's my house?"

"You travelled along the sparkle path, through the Prima Archway, and now you're here," replied the fairy, as if the whole thing was obvious.

"But…but where's here?!" stammered Faye.

"Here is Octavia," started the fairy. "My name is Forlana, by the way."

Just then, there was another rustling among the flowers and out popped a second fairy!

"Forlana, you're not making a very good job of this, you know," scolded the new fairy. He was taller and fairer than the girl, and had a mop of pale blonde hair.

"I'm doing my best," said Forlana crossly, "but she keeps interrupting me with questions!"

"Of course she does; that's because she's scared!" The second fairy looked at Faye (who was looking a little scared by now) for a minute, then he said, "Sit down and I'll explain everything."

Faye sat down on the grass at his feet. "Yes, please," she said, looking up at him.

"Right! My name is Landler, and that" – he indicated the other fairy, who stood with her hands on her hips, looking sulky – "is Forlana. We're the Music Fairies of Octavia, and it was our turn to watch the Mezzo Meadow for any new arrivals…and here you are!"

"But how?!" wailed Faye. "One minute I'm at home, sitting at the piano, and the next thing, a load of sparkles appeared, I walked along them and…and somehow ended up here!"

"How did she see the sparkles?" Forlana asked Landler. "Humans can only see them, if…oh!" She paused as she caught sight of Faye's necklace. "THAT'S how!"

Landler saw Faye looked puzzled, so he said kindly, "You have a Clef Crystal."

"I do?" murmured Faye.

"Yes," replied Landler. "They're very rare. The Clef Crystal allows humans to see the Sparkle Path, and follow it through the Prima Arch to the Mezzo Meadow."

"What's metso?" asked Faye.

"It means –" began Forlana.

"Now, no more questions yet. Would you like to see Cadence Falls?" asked Landler.

"Cadence Falls?" Faye repeated, weakly.

"It's where we live," replied Landler. "Come on!" He grabbed Faye's right hand and pulled her up from the grass.

"Can we manage her between the two of us?" he asked Forlana.

"Of course," she replied scornfully, coming to Faye's left-hand side and grabbing her free hand. "Ready, on three!"

"Where…?" began Faye, but as Forlana said "Three!" she suddenly felt herself being jerked upwards, her feet left the ground, and she was… FLYING!

"Aaah!" yelled Faye. "Put me down!"

"Now?!" asked Forlana sweetly, getting ready to let go.

"Don't you dare, Forlana!" Landler said sternly.

"Oh, you're no fun, Landler…As if I'd really drop her…yet," But Forlana took a firmer grip on Faye, as they flew higher.

Faye had kept her eyes tightly shut ever since her feet had left the ground, but after a little while, she sensed they were beginning to fly down, so she ventured to open her eyes just a little, and then saw something that made her forget all about being up in the air!

Just ahead was a little winding street, with small, neat, prettily painted houses on either side of it. Some had little flower beds in front, showing beautiful blooms in a myriad of colours. Others had little rock pools, with gnomes fishing at the edge of the water, but what Faye noticed most of all was at the end of the street. Trees had taken over from the houses, and nestled in amongst them was the most beautiful waterfall that Faye had ever seen! Faye decided there must be some sort of cliff behind the water, but she couldn't really see it, for the branches of the trees criss-crossed overhead, blocking her view.

As they began their descent, Faye noticed what appeared to be a shiny black fish diving in and out of the cascade. It only took her a couple of minutes to see all this, then the two fairies were gently lowering her into the street.

"This," Forlana said proudly, "is Cadence Falls."

"Wow!" said Faye, as she looked around. She'd just opened her mouth to ask another question when a beautiful clear note sounded somewhere above their heads; the fairies sang the same note back to the singer (who Faye couldn't see) and then several things happened at once.

All the garden gnomes (whom Faye had thought were ornaments) suddenly started running towards the waterfall. 'I wonder if they're going for a swim?' thought Faye, but suddenly they all turned to the right and disappeared from view.

Next, Forlana and Landler hurried Faye to a little wooden bench outside one of the houses.

"Stay here," said Landler. "We don't want you getting squished on your first day here!"

Faye sat down. She didn't understand what was happening, but she didn't like the idea of 'squished' so she obeyed.

All at once the gnomes returned with little gold wheelbarrows and nets. They went right up to the water's edge and began scooping up the shiny black fish in their nets. When they were full, the nets were emptied into the wheelbarrows.

Faye only had time to watch this happen once or twice before there was a great whirring sound, and the street and the air above it was filled with dozens of fairies!

They flew, they ran, they skipped and jumped; they called merrily to each other, all in a state of great excitement. Each fairy carried a small, round silver barrel, with an odd design engraved all the way round the top edge.

Faye couldn't imagine what these barrels were for, until she saw each fairy hover over the wheelbarrows until they could swoop down, fill their barrels with fish and then fly away again.

Soon the flurry of activity was over; the water ran clear again, and the fairies collected the last of the fish and took them away.

The gnomes went back to fishing in their gardens as if nothing had happened, and the waterfall cascaded down as gently as before.

Faye was so entranced by all this that she hadn't noticed when Forlana and Landler had disappeared. It wasn't until Landler flew down and stood in front of her, that she realised they'd been gone!

"Sorry about that," said Landler. "But when a cluster comes in like that, we have to grab them, otherwise…" He frowned, then shook himself and smiled. "What is your name?" he asked.

"Faye," she replied.

"Well, Faye," said Landler, as Forlana flew down to join them, "why don't you come back with us to my house, and Forlana and I will try to explain everything."

CHAPTER 5

As they sat in Landler's cosy cottage, sipping raspberry cordial out of acorn cups, Landler began. "As I said, Faye, we are Music Fairies. Our main job is to collect any stray music that appears in the waterfall, before…well, never mind that now. Our other job is to look out for humans wearing Clef Crystals in the Mezzo Meadow."

"What is metso?"

"It means 'in the middle'. It's a place that's between your world and ours."

"Oh," Faye shook her head. "But I still don't understand; you said, 'stray music'…like dogs at Battersea?"

"What's a 'Battersea'?" asked Forlana.

"It's a human place where lost animals go," Landler told her.

"Oh." Forlana looked blank.

"Now," continued Landler, "the stray notes, or 'Dots' as we call them, arrive when a human composer who's writing a song or symphony decides they don't like it, or it isn't good enough, and so they screw up the paper and throw it away. The unwanted Dots then come to Octavia and it's the gnomes' job to collect them from Cadence Falls, so we fairies can make sure they're reused properly."

"Recycling!" cried Faye, glad to find something she knew about in this unusual world. "My mum has a bin for that!"

"Bin?" echoed Forlana. "Battersea? You humans use such strange words!"

"I'm sure Faye will find some of our words strange, too!" laughed Landler. "We can teach each other!"

"But about the necklace," said Faye, bringing them back to the point. "It isn't even mine, not really. It belongs to my Great Aunt Laura – she only gave it to me three weeks ago!"

"THREE WEEKS!" cried Landler, in astonishment. He looked at Forlana. "She is going to be very powerful," he said, quietly.

"Most humans take a year or more before they find their way here,"

Forlana said, in awe.

"I didn't exactly find my way," murmured Faye awkwardly. "I got cross because I couldn't play 'Twinkle, Twinkle Little Star' with the right fingers, and so…I hit the piano really hard and…and the necklace suddenly started glowing," she finished quietly. Faye could see the two fairies were not impressed, so she hung her head.

"That's not the way to treat a piano," Landler said seriously. "You could damage it."

"Sorry, I know," sighed Faye, "but it's so HARD!"

"How long have you been having lessons?" asked Forlana.

"Three weeks!" groaned Faye.

"Three weeks?" squeaked Forlana. "Nobody can learn anything in three weeks! You have to practice!"

Faye looked stubborn and sulky. "I HATE that word! Mum uses it, Miss Hummingstone uses it, and even Great Aunt Laura says, 'Have you done your practice?'"

Landler smiled at her. "It's the only way to get better at anything. Incidentally, you're extremely lucky the Clef Crystal worked. It won't usually glow when people are angry; it must have sensed something special in you. Next time, try to be a bit more relaxed and happy."

"N…next time?" stuttered Faye in amazement. "There'll be a next time?"

"I should think so." Landler smiled. "The necklace brought you here for a purpose; we need to find out what it is."

A terrible thought struck Faye. "The notes! I don't know what I played. I can't remember! How will I find them again?"

"Oh, it's never the same notes twice," said Forlana airily. "The necklace ALWAYS knows when the time is right. Some people wear a Clef Crystal for years and nothing ever happens."

"Why not?" asked Faye.

"No one really knows," mused Landler. "Octavia only calls humans who can be of real help, those who have special gifts."

"I don't have any special gifts," muttered Faye.

"You must have," said Forlana reasonably, "or you wouldn't be here in the first place!"

"True!" agreed Landler. "But it will probably take some time before we find out what they are."

"What about Mum?" Faye cried suddenly. "She'll be worried when she can't find me – how long have I been gone?"

"Don't panic," said Forlana. "We've used the Façade Charm on her; she thinks you're still practising 'Twinkle, Twinkle'…" Forlana closed her eyes. "She can hear you from the kitchen."

"But supposing she comes in to watch?" said Faye.

Forlana and Landler smiled at each other, "She won't," they said in unison.

"Now, before you can think up any more problems, why don't you get some sleep and tomorrow we'll show you our little hamlet of Cadence Falls."

Forlana put out her hand, but as Faye took it and pulled herself up, a new problem presented itself.

"I can't be away all night! Mum won't believe I'm practising for eight hours!" Faye said indignantly.

"I'm sorry," replied Landler. "I didn't make it very clear. However long you spend in Octavia, only one hour will have elapsed in your world. EXACTLY one hour. So, you see, your mum will be very pleased you've done an hour's practice."

A delightful thought came into Faye's head. "Does this mean I won't have to actually practice any more?"

"Dear me, no!" said Forlana, shocked. "Of course you must practice! How will you ever get any better if you don't?"

"Oh," said Faye, crestfallen. "But...if Mum thinks I've been practising for an hour, how do I...you know...practice?"

"Don't worry, Faye." Landler smiled. "We'll explain all about that before you leave – it'll be fine."

"Now, come on!" insisted Forlana. "Off to sleep. We've loads to do tomorrow!"

Faye had to admit she was beginning to feel a bit sleepy, but she was also hungry, as she hadn't eaten for ages!

Landler seemed to realise this, because he came back with something in his hands. "I thought you might be hungry – I've only got apple cookies, I'm afraid, but I made them this morning, so they're fresh."

"Thank you!" said Faye, relieved. She bit into one, and it was the most delicious thing she'd ever tasted!

"It's yummy." She smiled.

"Thank you." Landler smiled back. "Now get some sleep."

Forlana led her to the back of the little cottage, and in a tiny room there was what looked like a walnut shell, filled with giant bird feathers! 'Of course it's not a REAL walnut shell,' thought Faye, 'because I wouldn't fit!'

"You can sleep here," Forlana whispered, and as Faye snuggled into the soft, downy feathers, she was asleep before she could ask Forlana, "What are we doing tomorrow?"

CHAPTER 6

The next day, after an excellent breakfast of scrambled eggs, toast and honey, the two fairies set off to show Faye around Cadence Falls.

"It's not very big," said Landler, modestly, "but we love it."

"It's very pretty," admired Faye, glancing around at all the pastel-coloured houses. Fairies popped their heads out of windows to wave or call out a greeting to Landler and Forlana (and some, quite frankly, just to stare at Faye!).

"Don't worry," said Landler when Faye noticed them, "every time a human crosses into Octavia, every fairy is curious to see what their gift will be."

"I've already told you I don't have a gift," said Faye quietly; "I'm not good at anything!"

"But –" began Forlana again.

"It's alright, Faye," Landler said with a pointed look at the other fairy. "Don't worry about it, just enjoy looking around."

"Okay," Faye sighed. She was certain that she'd been sent here by mistake. 'It should have been someone else,' she said to herself, 'not me!'

However, she did start to take more notice of her surroundings, and the one thing that really stood out was the curious fence.

She'd seen it yesterday, but with all the gnomes, wheelbarrows and fairies flying about, she hadn't really taken much notice of it. But now she looked and saw it wasn't really in keeping with the rest of the village. Cadence Falls was decorated in pretty pinks and lilacs, pale greens and blues, but this strange fence was dark, jet black, and looked very stern and forbidding!

There were five black rails set equally apart, and at regular intervals another stripe ran down the length of all five; the fence carried on and on, as far as the eye could see. Faye was just about to ask the fairies what the fence was for, when she noticed something else…the unpleasant-looking forest on the other side of the fence!

For a start the colours weren't pretty. The trees were murky green, as if they needed a good wash, and the ground, what little she could see of it, was a mess of khaki, black and brown; it looked muddy.

Faye didn't like the look of the forest at all! It reminded her of a nightmare she'd had once, where she was running and running, but her feet never got her anywhere. In the distance, above the trees, she could just make out a dark shape that looked black against the sky. It was too far away to tell whether it was a mountain, a castle, a tower or maybe…a giant!

Faye shivered.

"Come on," Forlana laughed. "Race you to the falls!"

The three of them ran down the lanes and streets, and eventually past the houses of the gnomes (not a wheelbarrow in sight), and reached the bank of the falls.

Forlana flopped down on the grass and trailed her hand in the clear water.

"Where does it go?" asked Faye.

"Who cares!" cried Forlana. "It's here, isn't it?"

"Yes," agreed Landler, patiently, "but Faye needs to know as much as she can about our world…eventually." He smiled at Faye. "The water comes from a mountain stream in your world and crosses over into ours by magic; the magic draws all the unwanted Dots into the water and sends them to Cadence Falls, where we can collect them. Then the water from the falls flows out into the Segue River, where magic takes it up to the mountain stream again."

"Wow!" said Faye, impressed. "That's clever!"

"Come on," cried Forlana, bored now, "there's someone I want you to meet."

"Who?" Landler looked doubtful. "She's only just got here; we don't want too much too soon, remember?"

"Meeting Polka won't hurt her," Forlana remarked casually, smoothing the pink petals of her skirt. "Besides, I want to see if my new dress is ready!"

"Oh, I see," Landler laughed. "Not so much for Faye's benefit, as yours!"

"Well, a bit of both really." Forlana smiled back. "Come on, Faye." The two of them ran off, leaving Landler to follow in their wake.

Forlana stopped at a pretty lemon-coloured house and leaned through the open window. "Polka! Are you in?"

The door opened and Faye saw a merry fairy dressed all in green, with big yellow circles all over her dress.

"Hello, Forlana," said Polka. "Who's this then?"

"This is Faye," Forlana said, pushing Faye forward. "She has a Clef Crystal," she added, as an afterthought.

"Of course she has, otherwise she wouldn't be here!" Polka laughed, shaking her head. "Hello, Faye, welcome to Cadence Falls."

"Thank you." Faye smiled shyly, wishing she was better at meeting new people.

"Come in, come in." Polka led the way into a neat little room. "Your dress is almost finished."

"Oh goody!" Forlana did a little prance round in her excitement. "I wondered if it was ready."

"I just need to hold it up to your shoulders and check the hem." Polka disappeared into the back room as she spoke and returned with a pretty, pale blue dress, decorated with silver sparkles around the top and hem.

"Ooh!" cried Faye and Forlana together. "That's the most beautiful dress!"

"Glad you like it." Polka smiled. "Let's just try it." She placed the dress against Forlana's shoulders. "Hold here, please, Forlana – that's right." Polka knelt down to see if the hem was straight. "Hmm…" She frowned. "There's a little bit I don't like – can you wait while I alter it?"

"Of course!" the girls cried.

"I'll put the kettle on, then." Polka fluttered into the kitchen, where they soon heard the clattering of teacups.

"Isn't it gorgeous?" said Forlana, admiring the dress (and herself) in a mirror which stood by the wall.

"Beautiful!" Faye sighed, wishing she could have something that pretty. She loved dressing up at home, although she was far too shy to go to a fancy-dress party.

"By the way, where's Landler?" called Polka from the kitchen. Faye looked round for the other fairy.

"He's probably waiting outside; he's not very interested in Fairy Fashion," Forlana said, as if she couldn't understand anyone not being interested!

Polka laughed. "Go and see if he wants some tea, would you, Faye?"

Faye stepped outside and, sure enough, Landler was leaning against the wall.

"Still peering in the looking glass, is she?"

"Well," said Faye wistfully, "it is a very pretty dress. I'm to ask would you like some tea? Polka is just making it."

"Polka's Lupin tea? Definitely!" Landler pushed himself off the wall and strode inside, just as Polka was setting cups and saucers on the little oak table.

"Thought you'd be in for Lupin tea." Polka smiled. "Come and sit down."

"Thanks, Polka." He looked around the table. "Do you, by any chance, have some of those honey and chrysanthemum cakes to go with the tea?"

"Well…" said Polka, pretending to think, "I knew Forlana would be itching to see her dress, and I thought you might keep her company, so…I baked a fresh batch this morning!"

"Aah…" Landler stretched out in his chair. "You're a fairy of many talents, Polka!"

Polka returned from the kitchen with a beautiful blue and white china teapot, suspended from a bamboo handle, and a plate of little sunshine-yellow cakes with criss-crosses of honey drizzled on the top.

While her guests helped themselves, Polka went to her sewing basket to fetch a needle and thread, and was just about to sit down when Faye's "Ooh!" made her jump.

"What's wrong?" Polka asked in alarm.

"The t…tea!" Faye stuttered. "It's…it's…BLUE!"

"Of course it is," said Forlana. "What colour did you expect Lupin tea to be?"

"Um…it's just that tea is usually brown in my world," said Faye, not wanting to offend.

"How boring!" muttered Forlana.

"Rude!" Landler shot a look at her, and then said to Faye "You do have fruit teas, too, don't you?"

"I think so," Faye replied, "but not blue!"

"Actually, you do have blue tea." Polka smiled. "It's called 'blue chai' and it's made from butterfly pea flowers."

"Really?" Faye was amazed. "I've never heard of it. I'm sorry, Polka; your Lupin tea is lovely." She hastily drank some, and it was!

"Good." Polka smiled again. "Now, I must just alter this hem." She began unpicking the bottom of Forlana's dress and then proceeded to sew with such tiny stitches that Faye couldn't see them!

Finally she held the dress up for all to see. "There you are, Forlana, all finished."

"Thank you so much, Polka," said Forlana excitedly. "I can't wait to wear it!"

"Now there's a surprise!" Landler laughed, getting up. "Come on, you two, it's time we left."

They said goodbye to Polka and started to walk back towards the waterfall, Forlana carefully carrying her new dress.

"I wanted to ask you, what's that up there?" Faye said suddenly, pointing to the dark outline at the top of the forest.

"Oh, that's D —"

"Nothing for you to be concerned about, yet," Landler cut across whatever Forlana had been about to say, and she glared at him crossly. "Remember, not too much too soon," he said quietly.

"I don't understand; what are you two talking about?" cried Faye, feeling a bit left out.

"I tell you what," said Landler suddenly, changing the subject, "why don't we show Faye the Blackberry Lanes and we can pick some for our supper?"

"Ooh, I love blackberries!" Faye cheered up at once.

"Come on, then," sighed Forlana. "We'd better stop at yours for some baskets, though."

"Of course." Landler smiled. "You can leave your dress there, too."

"I only live next door," Forlana said indignantly. "I'll leave my dress there, thank you very much."

"Oh, well, in that case," said Landler, with a wink at Faye, "we can use your baskets."

"What, and get them all stained with blackberry juice? No thanks! We'll use yours!"

They spent the afternoon picking the biggest, juiciest blackberries Faye had ever seen, and by the time they had finished, all three of them were covered in dark purple juice!

"I think we'd better get cleaned up before we go home," said Landler ruefully.

"Let's go to the Pizzicato Pool. I love it there," cried Forlana.

"Very well," Landler replied.

They arrived to find the pool full of laughing, swimming fairies.

"This is a magic pool, of course," said Forlana in a superior tone, "so the water can't damage our wings," and she dived in. "Remember, Faye, we're of magic, but we don't use magic."

Faye paddled at the water's edge, too embarrassed to admit she couldn't swim.

"Come on!" yelled Forlana. "It's lovely and warm!"

"It's alright," said Landler quietly to her. "You'll be able to swim here, even if you can't at home – it's magic, remember?"

"How did you know?"

"Not the first human to come here!" Landler laughed, taking her hand and diving in.

Faye expected to come up coughing and spluttering, but to her delight, she found she could swim easily.

"This is great!" she cried happily.

After they'd splashed about for a while, she suddenly saw all the fairies stop and look towards the far shore, so she paddled her feet and watched too.

All at once, the water started to bubble and ripple, as up to the surface rose twenty or so pale green figures. Each carried a small harp, and, at a sign from their leader, they all began to play.

As they plucked the strings of their harps the most beautiful music floated in the air. All the fairies were completely still, entranced by the sound, and Faye thought about rainbows and unicorns while the harps played.

All too soon the music stopped, and the pale green harpists disappeared beneath the waters once more.

"What…what was that?" whispered Faye in awe.

"That," Landler whispered back, "was the Ondulandi – the rippling water sprites. They live at the bottom of the pool and, once a day, they come up to serenade us with their harps."

"That's why it's called the Pizzicato Pool!" burst out Forlana, tired of being ignored. "It means to pluck, you know, like twanging the strings?"

"Thank you, Forlana," sighed Landler, the tranquil mood completely broken now.

They went back to Landler's and stuffed themselves full of blackberries and cream, after which Forlana went next door, put on her new dress and returned to show it off to the others.

Faye managed two 'It's lovely!'s before she began to yawn, too full of blackberries to stay awake.

Landler noticed. "Bed," he said, and Faye nodded sleepily.

As she snuggled down, her last waking thought was, 'Oh, bother – I forgot to ask about the fence!'

Was it to keep the fairies in…or something else out?

CHAPTER 7

The following morning there was a great bustle of activity in Cadence Falls. Faye was woken up by an old gnome shouting up and down the street, "Blackcurrant polish! Blackcurrant polish! Don't forget to polish your shoes for this afternoon!"

She ran to the window and looked out; fairies were fluttering about, carrying pretty dresses or smart tunics over their arms and holding their best shoes. Several stopped by the old gnome for polish, then flew off balancing that as well!

Gnomes were washing their windows and singing while they polished up the handles of their small front doors.

Faye ran to the kitchen and asked, "What's going on?"

Landler looked up from the large pan where he was cooking eggs and mushrooms. "Why, it's the festival this afternoon – in all the excitement of your arrival, I forgot to tell you!"

"Festival?" queried Faye.

"Yes! Festival!" repeated Forlana impatiently, who was stood by the table. "What did you think my new dress was for?"

"I...I don't know," stuttered Faye, aware that she'd somehow made the fairy cross.

"Leave her alone, Forlana," warned Landler. "How's she supposed to know?"

Forlana sat down with a sigh. "Very well. It's a celebration. All the folk from miles around come to the Cadence Falls Fairy Festival. It simply has EVERYTHING! There are stalls selling drinks and cakes and necklaces and clothes. There are games and races and, later, a competition for the best dressed fairy!"

Faye looked at Landler as Forlana gave out the last piece of information; they both smiled, for they knew she expected to win!

"...And then," continued Forlana, "there's a party with music, singing and dancing to finish with."

"It all sounds wonderful," sighed Faye. She would have loved to have gone, but she was wearing her old jeans and the pink T-shirt with the cat on it – hardly party wear!

However, Landler seemed to guess the problem as he served them breakfast. "Forlana," he began after he'd swallowed a huge mouthful of scrambled egg, "what do you do with all your 'old' dresses – you know, the ones you've worn at least twice?"

"Those?" Forlana frowned. "I don't know, they're probably in a chest somewhere – why?"

"Well," replied Landler, with a significant nod towards Faye, "I thought it might be nice if we took Faye to the festival, seeing as she's never been…" he paused.

"Okay, she can come," murmured Forlana carelessly.

"Yes…but she'll need something to wear…" Landler left the sentence open.

Faye, who had been listening avidly to their conversation, held her breath.

Forlana looked up at Landler, who pointedly looked back at her.

"What? But…oh, alright then…she can borrow one of my older dresses!" Forlana looked Faye up and down. "Her figure's different to mine!" she said, as if she'd only just realised.

"That's because she's a human child!" Landler explained patiently. He stood up. "You choose one of your 'older' dresses, and I'll take Faye to Polka's and have her alter it to fit."

"Oh, very well." Forlana fluttered off to her house next door, where she could be heard rummaging about.

"I don't want to be a nuisance to Polka," whispered Faye to Landler, "especially when she's so busy."

"Don't you worry about that." Landler smiled. "She'll have it fixed in a jiffy."

Forlana came back with a dress folded over one arm.

"Here", she thrust it at Faye, "I don't know if it will fit, but it's the only one I really can't bear to wear again – I never liked it!"

Faye held the dress out and looked at it. "It's…it's…"

"Yes, hideous, isn't it?" Forlana said.

"Beautiful!" sighed Faye, admiring the soft lilac and pale green shimmering folds.

"Really?!" squeaked Forlana. "But…green and lilac? I don't know what possessed me…oh well, if you really like it that much…you can have it… as a present," she added magnanimously.

Faye smiled and said thank you so many times that Landler whisked her and the dress off to Polka's after the fifth 'Thank you'!

"She'll want to spend the rest of the morning getting ready, if I know Forlana," Landler said.

Polka took one quick look at the dress, another at Faye, then got her tape measure out and jotted some numbers down.

"Right," she said briskly, "I'm going to have to add some more material to the waist and find something to cover the wing-slits at the back, but it shouldn't take too long. If you'll both sit down, I'll just put the kettle…"

A sudden harsh sound filled the air, making Faye clap her hands over her ears. The two fairies looked at each other, and Faye thought they seemed just a little bit…afraid.

The sound got suddenly louder, and Faye screamed, "The waterfall! There's something wrong at the waterfall!"

Dozens of fairies streamed past Polka's open door; the gnomes, too, were running.

"How does she know?" Polka asked Landler in dismay.

"Never mind how – she does!" he said. "Faye," Landler turned to face her, "we fairies need your help. Something terrible is about to happen and I think you're the only one who can stop it."

"M…me?" Faye was horrified. "B…but how…?"

Just then the awful noise stopped, and Faye realised she'd been shouting.

"Quick," cried Landler, "Polka, grab her other hand; I need her at the falls NOW!"

Without any warning, Faye found herself dragged outside and up, up into the air. She could see the reason for this at once; the ground was so crowded with fairies, gnomes and wheelbarrows that they would never have got through on foot.

"Look!" yelled Landler, pointing with his free hand. Faye looked and finally saw what all the fuss was about.

The waterfall no longer looked like water; instead it was a heaving, moving mass of black, like the worst swarm of flies she'd ever seen, during one particularly hot summer.

"What's happening?" she cried to Landler.

"It's a Dot Deluge," he replied grimly. "Somewhere in the human world, a composer is having a meltdown. He's ripping apart page after page of music in anger. The Dots are rejected and full of dark emotion, and if too many Dots come at once, the falls can't cope, and we have a Deluge! We must collect up every single Dot and calm them down, otherwise…"

"Otherwise what?" asked Faye, but they were already landing near the foot of the falls and the noise was incredible!

People shouting, wheelbarrows flying back and forth, Dots jumping with angry bounces out of the waterfall, landing on the street and rolling away in all directions.

"Quick!" shouted Landler. "Some of you stand guard at the Bar Barriers – don't let any of them through!"

A few of the taller, stronger-looking fairies moved off down a little winding path to the left and disappeared out of sight.

"Tell me what to do!" yelled Faye, feeling that she ought to be doing something.

"Here, grab this!" Polka thrust an acorn bowl into her hands. "Collect them carefully; when your bowl is full, give it to one of the gnomes, but don't touch the water!" With that she went, and Faye saw her giving similar bowls to younger fairies who were unsure on how best to help. Faye picked up a couple of Dots by her feet. To her surprise, they were hot and buzzed against her hand; she put them in the bowl quickly.

"NOT WITH YOUR HANDS!" A fairy in red dashed over to her. "Here. Use a scoop!" He pushed one at her.

Landler was flying just above everyone's heads, shouting instructions and warnings as fairies began to get injured.

"Right!" he yelled. "All fairies STEP BACK from the falls – let the gnomes through; if your wings get badly singed you won't be able to fly again – EVER!"

All the fairies moved back hastily, and Faye could see that some of them had tiny burn-holes at the tips of their wings, where the water had splashed them. A fairy in white and blue was dabbing some ointment on the burns, then moving onto the next fairy.

"What's burning them?" Faye asked a fairy, who was skipping back out of the way.

"The rejection of the Dots reacts with the water; when there are so many of them, the water becomes like acid and it burns."

Faye stepped back quickly; she had no wings to burn, but she'd touched Mum's iron once and she still remembered how much it had hurt!

She filled her bowl and fought her way through to the nearest gnome, who emptied the Dots into his wheelbarrow, then gave her the bowl back.

With Landler in charge, things got more organised now. The gnomes made good use of the space left by the fairies, and before long, there was a steady rhythm of, "SPADE, BARROW, SPADE, BARROW, FULL, TURN, WHEEL, UNLOAD, TURN, WHEEL

BACK AGAIN."

Faye and the Music Fairies scooped up as much as they could into their acorn bowls, tipped them into the wheelbarrows, and the gnomes then emptied them into large barrels that seemed to have appeared all by themselves, until Faye spotted a couple of strong-looking younger gnomes rolling away the full barrels and replacing them with empty ones.

As time went on, Faye began to realise two things. Everyone was starting to get tired, and therefore slower, but the Dot Deluge showed no signs of stopping. In fact, if anything it was getting bigger! Faye didn't know how much longer they could go on. She looked up for Landler and spotted him a few feet above her, near the falls, looking exhausted.

She was about to call him to come down and rest for a bit, when there was an ominous roar in the distance. It grew louder and came nearer.

Landler spun round in mid-air to see a new, vicious black wave come hurtling towards him, over the edge of the falls!

It hit Landler where he flew and sent him tumbling down, to land a few feet away from Faye…so completely covered in angry Dots that Faye could barely see his face.

He lay quite still.

CHAPTER 8

"Landler!" Faye screamed, as several gnomes converged on him, removing the Dots as fast as they could.

By the time Faye reached him she could see he was very pale and his eyes were shut.

Faye knelt down and touched his arm. "Landler." She shook him gently. "Landler!" Nothing.

Suddenly there was a commotion behind them.

"Out of the way – let me through!" Forlana pushed the last group of fairies apart and ran towards Faye.

"What happened?"

"There was a huge wave and…and…" Faye sobbed quietly.

"…it hit him," finished Forlana grimly.

She knelt on the other side of Landler and took out a small bottle from a pouch at her waist. She opened it and poured a small amount into Landler's mouth.

"Vivace drops," she muttered to Faye, "they should revive him."

Faye watched as Landler slowly opened his eyes and blinked, trying to clear his vision. She glanced at Forlana, hoping she would say 'There you are – all better', when she saw the fairy was crying too.

Landler tried to sit up…and failed.

"Take it easy." Forlana smiled through her tears. "You just lost a fight with the Deluge!"

"I know," replied Landler weakly. "Come on, sis, cheer up – I'll be okay."

"You'd better be, big brother, or I'll get saddled with looking after you!"

Faye gasped; she hadn't realised that the two fairies were brother and sister, but now she looked at them both, she could see they did resemble each other a little.

Just then, four of the guard fairies ran up. The first said, "Landler, we…" He stopped, seeing his leader was injured.

"Over here." Forlana got to her feet. "Stay with him, Faye."

Forlana beckoned the guards to one side and they followed her. She then sent two of them in opposite directions.

Faye watched them having what looked like a very serious discussion.

"I think I know what they're saying," said Landler in a strained voice. "Listen, Faye…I wanted to take the time to teach you properly, one step at a time, but it looks as though I'm going to have to ask you to be brave… to take a dark and dangerous journey to save ALL the music fairies."

"M…me?" stuttered Faye in disbelief. (She still slept with a night light on, sometimes, but she wasn't about to admit that to Landler!) "But…but I'm not brave or anything, and…and I wouldn't know what to do!"

"You'll have help," gasped Landler, before he lay back again, exhausted.

Faye was panicking; she didn't want to leave Landler, who looked terrible again, and she was scared witless about the 'dark and dangerous journey', but on the other hand, she couldn't leave all her new friends to be destroyed!

"Right!" Forlana's voice cut across her thoughts, as two fairies in blue and white came over to Landler. "You two carry Landler to his house, and you two, put him to bed and tend to him. GENTLY!" She glared at the two guards who knelt to pick Landler up as gently as possible.

They flew off slowly, with the medic fairies supporting his head and his feet.

"Polka!" cried Forlana, looking around her in agitation, and then sighing with relief as she spotted the fairy.

"Will you stay with Landler until I can get back?"

"Of course I will." Polka gave Forlana's hand a squeeze and flew off after the group carrying him.

Forlana watched them go, then took a deep breath and turned to Faye.

"I need you to come with me now, not to ask too many questions, and…" she looked and Faye with worried eyes, "…I need…Landler needs you to be the bravest you've ever been; do you think you can?"

Faye, who had never been clever, or brave, or particularly good at anything, drew herself up and said, "I'll do my best."

"That's all anyone can ask," responded Forlana. "Come on then, follow me!"

They weaved their way through the fairies who were still cleaning up the mess left by the Deluge, and the gnomes gathering the remaining Dots.

Landler hadn't been the only one to be hit by the last massive wave, and Faye saw a group of gnomes taking two of their kind off in wheelbarrows; one looked as if his leg was broken.

"I need to explain a couple of things as we go," said Forlana, briskly, as they passed the main crowd, "but please, PLEASE don't interrupt or ask questions till I'm finished."

"Alright," replied Faye, fearfully sure there would be many questions and hoping she could manage NOT to ask them!

Forlana pulled Faye down a smaller lane to their right that led downhill; it was quieter here, so Forlana began.

"We Music Fairies have many different jobs to perform, but the single most important task we can ever do is to make sure no Dots ever escape from Cadence Falls into the Cacophony Woods."

Faye opened her mouth.

"Don't ask what cacophony means – I'll tell you later!" exclaimed Forlana crossly.

Faye shut her mouth.

"We've only had two Deluges that I can remember," continued Forlana, "and both times we managed to contain almost every single Dot. But today," Forlana shivered, "there were too many of them, and some of the Dots got past the guards and have escaped into the woods!"

Forlana shot Faye a quick look and Faye sighed, the question she had been about to ask disappearing in the air.

"The Bar Barrier that runs all the way round Cadence Falls is there for two reasons. One of them doesn't concern us yet, but the other is to stop anything or anyone from the Cacophony Woods getting in here. The Bar lines are full of magic, which usually works. But with such a massive number of Dots, the guards couldn't collect them fast enough, so several swarms have got into the woods and will soon be under the spell of an evil witch, who will try to make them come to her. If that happens, she will use them to create a terrible force that drains all the love and happiness out of music; she'll turn them into Discords!"

Faye didn't know what a Discord was, but it didn't sound very good!

Forlana went on, "We fairies cannot cross the Bar Barrier; the hatred and noise is too strong for a fairy to bear, we simply…cease to exist!"

"No!" Faye shouted. She put her hand over her mouth, but Forlana didn't seem to have noticed.

"Only a human can go into the Cacophony Woods and survive. That's why we use the Clef Crystals to search for humans who can help us in times of trouble."

Faye swallowed hard. She really hoped the fairies weren't going to pin all their hopes on her! She started to form a question but then stopped as she realised they had been walking to a part of Cadence Falls she'd not seen, and to her surprise, two of the guard fairies were there before them!

Faye had thought they'd left all the fairies behind.

"Right, you two!" Forlana strode up to them. "I need you to fly Faye to the Red Barn."

"Yes, Forlana," Souza, the older guard, said.

Forlana turned to Faye. "This is going to be a bit uncomfortable, because it's a longer journey than the last two, but I need you to get there quickly!"

"Okay," said Faye in a small voice, as the two guards took hold of her hands.

"I'm coming with you, but we won't be able to talk on the journey; I need to concentrate on flying. I'll answer all your questions when we get to the Red Barn, alright?"

Faye nodded, as the guards counted 'one, two' and on 'three!' she felt herself being lifted up. Forlana flew just ahead of them.

Faye had plenty of time to think about what Forlana had told her as they flew along.

She discovered the drag on her arms didn't hurt as much if she concentrated on other things. (Her arms, which had begun to get a bit sore after a while, were now positively painful!) So she thought about what Landler and Forlana could possibly expect her to do for the Music Fairies. She didn't know anything about music – not really. She could recognise some of the notes…quavers and crotchets, but she couldn't play. 'Why didn't the Clef Crystal bring someone who could play?' thought Faye. It just didn't make any sense.

Suddenly, after they'd flown for what seemed like ages, Faye could see buildings in the distance. 'Maybe it's another village,' Faye thought. 'I hope we're landing soon.'

She peered down for a better look. Instead of the pretty little houses of Cadence Falls, Faye now saw some big wooden buildings that reminded her of the barns she'd visited on a school trip to a farm.

Forlana flew in the direction of the largest barn, painted bright red, and standing apart from all the others; they followed her. As soon as they landed, Forlana led the way into the building.

Once they were inside, Faye stopped in surprise, for she couldn't quite believe what she was seeing!

A large and very beautiful red, orange and gold butterfly was standing in the centre of the floor, while fairies flew round it, spraying the gorgeous fragile-looking wings with green, brown and black paint!

"Stop!" gasped Faye in horror. "You'll damage his wings! He won't be able to fly!"

"Don't worry," said the butterfly. Faye nearly fell over, she was so surprised! "I'm not quite the same as the butterflies you have in your world."

"No, ours don't talk," Faye blurted out.

"Yes, they do!" snapped Forlana. "You just can't hear them with your stupid human ears!"

"For-LANA!" snapped one of the painting fairies flying over to them.

"Oh...I'm sorry, Faye. I'm just..." She stopped in mid-sentence and flew off to the doors of the barn where she could be heard, ordering the guards back to Cadence Falls.

"Never mind her." The fairy who was covered in splashes of paint smiled. "We've heard about Landler; she must be worried sick. I'm Rollo, by the way."

"I'm Faye."

"I know!" replied Rollo. "We've all been told about your arrival!"

"Have you?" Faye was still bothered by the amount of attention she was attracting.

"Oh yes, and now we know why you're here, we've been getting Brio ready for you." He smiled, indicating the butterfly.

"F...for...m...me?" Faye looked at the butterfly, who was a little larger than a small car, by human terms!

"What am I supposed to do with him?" she whispered.

"Why, fly him of course!" Rollo laughed. "However did you think you were going to get around the Cacophony Woods?"

"Um...well..." Faye let the sentence fade away; everyone was treating her as though she knew what she was doing, as though this was an everyday thing – flying on a giant butterfly, saving a whole race of fairies! What WAS she going to do?

As if he sensed her anxiety, Rollo took her hand. "Why don't we get you something to eat and drink while Brio's wings are drying?" He smiled, leading her to a small table with three stools round it. There was a jug and a plate of little cakes in the centre.

"Help yourself," called Rollo, as he went to fetch more plates and some mugs.

"There's no set mealtimes here," he told her as he returned. "We just come and eat whenever we have the time."

Rollo sat opposite Faye and poured her a mug of...

"Lupin tea!" exclaimed Faye.

"I see you've met Polka!" Rollo laughed. "Yes, she grows enough Lupins in her garden for the whole of Cadence Falls!"

Faye sipped her tea and ate a few of the cakes. She slowly began to feel a bit calmer, and when Forlana joined them, subdued and a bit red-eyed, she smiled at the fairy.

"Sorry, Faye," said Forlana quietly. "I was rude before. I didn't mean it – it's just with Landler – "

"I know," Faye cut in quickly. "Look, you've brought me here now, so why don't you go back and see Landler?"

"What? And have him never forgive me for leaving you before the mission? No thanks!" She gave Faye a weak smile to take the sting out of her words.

"Talking of the mission," broke in Rollo, "have you explained to Faye exactly what it is we need her to do?"

"Not yet; I was sort of building up to it," Forlana reluctantly replied. "It's an awful lot to ask of a human and she's very young."

"I know," said Rollo gently, "but she was sent for a reason. Come on, Forlana – Faye appears and a few days later we have the first Deluge for years? That can't be a coincidence."

"I am still here!" Faye said crossly, wondering when they would start talking to her instead of about her!

"Sorry, Faye," said Rollo, "we're just a bit concerned about you, that's all."

"Thank you," replied Faye, "but please can someone tell me what it is I'm supposed to do?"

"Of course." Rollo placed his elbows on the table and pressed the fingertips of each hand together.

"What we need you to do, Faye, is to collect up every Dot that has escaped into the Cacophony Woods and send them back to us, before they fall into the hands of Dee Sharp!"

CHAPTER 9

The barn suddenly went quiet.

"Who…who's Dee Sharp?" Faye whispered into the silence.

Forlana sighed. "Dee Sharp is the witch who lives on the far side of Cacophony Woods."

"In the castle at the top of the hill!" cried Faye suddenly, remembering the black shape she had seen looming against the sky.

"That's right!" said Forlana, giving Faye a strange glance. "She hates all music: all singers, all musicians and especially ALL composers! Every time a composer destroys a piece he or she has written, Dee Sharp casts an enchantment to call all the discarded Dots to her. Out of them she creates the Discords."

At this moment, a fairy ran up to Rollo, whispered something in his ear and then the two of them left, fetching Brio on the way.

"What are Discords?" asked Faye.

"The Discords," an older fairy with silver hair, called Lesto, took up the story, "are the chief weapons of Dee Sharp. She uses them to destroy whatever beautiful music she can find; every Discord she creates makes her that much stronger!"

Faye had a sinking feeling in the pit of her stomach. "What would happen if she got really strong?"

Lesto looked Faye squarely in the face. "She could destroy all music – not just in our world, but in yours too!"

"No!" gasped Faye; she couldn't imagine a world with no music! Mum wouldn't be able to sing along to the car CD, Faye's favourite band wouldn't be able to play and Miss Hummingstone wouldn't have anything to teach. It would be terrible!

Faye took a deep, slow breath. "What do I have to do?"

Lesto smiled. "Good girl. That's the spirit."

"Now, listen carefully." Forlana's strident tones were back. "Once you cross into the Cacophony Woods, we can't help you, so it's really important to remember what we are telling you now!"

"Alright," said Faye. "I'm listening."

"You will fly Brio…"

"What? But…"

"I thought you said you were listening," snapped Forlana, angrily.

"B…but…" faltered Faye, "apart from the guards just now, the only flying I've done was with you and Landler…and then with Polka," she remembered. "I've never done it on my own!"

"Don't be stupid – you won't be doing the flying, Brio will. How else did you think you were going to be able to cross the Cacophony Woods?"

"Forlana." Rollo had come back without them noticing; he spoke quietly, but Faye heard the anger in his voice. "Do you want Faye to help us or not?"

Forlana looked up at Rollo, and then at Faye. "I'm sorry…I can't do this." She got up and ran from the table. Rollo signalled Lesto to go after her, and Faye saw the two of them leave the barn.

"Now, Faye," said Rollo kindly, "Brio will fly you, because if you touch anything in the forest, the evil and anger that dwells there will enter your mind and make you so sad and unhappy that you will never find your way out again!"

"Oh!" gasped Faye, horrified.

"So…" continued Rollo, "we will give you a special device, called a Tremolo Vox Box; it has a long handle which will allow you to capture the Dots without setting foot in the Cacophony Woods. Once you have them you press a little button and the Dots are magically transported to the gnomes, who put them in the Danger Barrels."

"I've seen them do that!" recalled Faye.

"Exactly!" replied Rollo. "The gnomes have much tougher skin than us fairies, or indeed humans, so they can normally deal with the Dots without getting hurt…unless there's a Deluge."

Faye nodded, remembering the injured gnomes she had seen.

"The problem is," Rollo continued, "that we don't know exactly how many Dots escaped, so we won't know if you've caught them all or not."

"But then, how…?"

"Don't worry about it, Faye. Every Dot you capture is one less for Dee Sharp to use in her evil plans; it's a constant battle."

He sounded so serious as he said this that Faye wondered, for the hundredth time, why she had been chosen to deal with this problem. She had a horrible feeling that she might let everyone down!

A fairy dressed all in red, came up to them. "Rollo, we've just checked Brio over and he's dry now, and saddled, so we're all set."

"Thanks. Come on then, Faye, let's get you ready." Rollo stood up.

Faye tugged at his sleeve, whispering, "How's Brio going to fly if his wings are all stuck together with paint?"

"He'll manage." Rollo laughed. "He always does!"

"He's done this before?" asked Faye, aghast, as they began to walk.

"Of course – he's a Beamer Butterfly!"

Faye had no idea what that was, so she went on, "But why does he have to be painted?"

"Camouflage!" Rollo seemed surprised she'd had to ask. "You'll both need to blend in with the woods; you'd be a nice target otherwise!"

"Both...? You're not going to paint me, too, are you?"

"Of course not." Rollo laughed. "Here you are." They'd reached the next building by this time; a large shed with a green roof. As they entered Brio was waiting for them and a fairy was holding out a long, dingy-coloured coat with a hood attached.

"Put this on," said Rollo.

Faye did so, as another fairy came up with a strange collection of tubes, straps and nets, with a box at one end and a long handle at the other. "Here we are – your Tremolo Vox Box," he said, smiling at her. "Press the silver button to open the box," he did so, and Faye saw a trapdoor at the bottom of the box spring open, "and the gold button for transportation to the gnomes. DON'T mix them up!"

"Right," said Faye, faintly.

A ladder on a stand was being wheeled towards her. It stopped at Brio's side and the butterfly dipped his wing.

"Up you go!" cried Rollo, cheerfully.

Faye had just set one foot on the bottom rung, when Forlana rushed in.

"Stop!" she cried. Faye turned to look at her. "Faye, Landler would want me to give you this." Forlana handed Faye the pouch she kept on her belt, from which Faye had seen her take the tiny bottle when Landler was injured.

Forlana went on, "It contains the Vivace Drops; three will make you feel stronger for a little while, some food and...my Sprite-Force Amulet."

"No!" cried Rollo, as the other fairies gasped. "You can't! Without your Sprite-Force Amulet, you'll have no protection against any evil magic!"

"Landler would have given her his – he would want her to have it!" Forlana repeated fiercely. "Listen, Faye, I don't know if any of this will work for humans, but it's all I have!"

"Thank you, Forlana." Faye realised, as she took the pouch and tucked it safely inside a pocket of the coat, that this was a really big sacrifice the fairy was making for her, and, somehow, Forlana's faith in her made her feel stronger.

"I won't let you all down! Tell Landler I said that, please."

Forlana and Rollo smiled at each other and then at Faye.

"We knew you wouldn't!" stated Rollo.

The fairies watched as Faye climbed the ladder and found the saddle straps awaiting her on Brio's back. She strapped herself in, flung the Tremolo Vox Box across one shoulder, took a deep breath and said, "Ready, Brio? Let's go!"

CHAPTER 10

It was all very well, thought Faye as she flew along on Brio's back, to promise not to let the Music Fairies down when she was safe, warm and dry in the barn, and quite another thing when she was cold, wet and afraid, flying further into danger every minute! They'd been travelling all night, and now it was what passed for dawn, but what with the murky fog and persistent drizzle, Faye doubted they'd find so much as one Dot any time soon!

"Are you okay, Brio?" Faye suddenly wondered how far the butterfly would be able to carry her before he needed a rest, and then…where would they land?

"I'm fine, thanks, Faye," replied Brio. As if he guessed her thoughts, he added, "I don't tire easily, you know."

Brio sounded positively cheerful and Faye realised, for the first time since they'd left Cadence Falls, that she'd been getting more and more miserable.

"Brio," she said shyly, "can the Cacophony Woods make humans miserable, even if they're not touching it?"

"Of course!" Brio sounded surprised. "Didn't they teach you about it before you left?"

"Well, Landler said that he was going to explain it all slowly, bit by bit, you know, but then there was the Deluge, and Landler…" Faye broke off, tears stinging her eyes as she remembered Landler lying very still, covered in angry Dots…

"Stop that!" Brio's sharp reprimand cut across her thoughts. "That's exactly how Dee Sharp wants you to feel. A little more and we might as well give up now and go home!"

Faye was shocked and a little hurt by the butterfly's tone; she'd thought they were becoming friends, but she took a deep breath and said, "Sorry, Brio. I'll try not to get sad again."

"Good girl," Brio's voice was infused with approval and Faye felt better.

She was just about to ask Brio where they were heading next, when he suddenly swerved and she clutched at the straps.

"Quick, Faye – get the Tremolo Vox Box ready; I can see Dots!"

How he could see them Faye didn't know, but she obeyed and took the strap off her shoulder. She could just make out the panel which said 'Press' on the side of the handle. She pressed it and the long wooden handle became even longer as it extended down into the murky gloom.

On the side of the handle, near the top, were the two buttons. 'Right,' she thought, 'silver for capture and gold for transportation.'

"Hold tight!" called Brio. "And have your hand ready over the silver button!"

Faye lifted her forefinger until it hovered over the button…and waited.

"Now!" Brio swooped down as he spoke and Faye pushed the button; a long silvery note sounded in the silence. Faye remembered the note she'd heard when she first came to Cadence Falls, but this note was different – it wobbled! That was the only way to describe it. The wobbling got bigger and bigger until Faye could feel it in the bones behind her ears.

Then suddenly, through the gloom, the air was full of angry, black, swirling shapes all around her head. The Dots were coming!

Afterwards, Faye said it was worse than being attacked by a swarm of wasps, but at the time, all she could do was to follow Brio's instructions. "Don't swat at them, Faye! They'll fly down to the nets, because that's where the note's coming from. Hold the box still! Right! When I say, press the gold button…ready? Go!"

Faye did as she was told, and immediately the note stopped singing and there was silence once more.

"Well done!" Faye was pleased to hear the approval in Brio's voice, but she had a question. "When I pressed the silver button back at the barn, there was no note – why?"

"Well, there wouldn't be, with no Dots to activate it, would there?"

"Oh," Faye sighed. She felt so unprepared for all of this. "I didn't know!"

"I know it's hard, Faye, when you haven't been taught properly and you can't see what you're doing, but you must learn to trust me, and we'll be fine!"

"I DO trust you, Brio," Faye hastily reassured him, "but there's still one thing I don't understand. How can you see down there when I can't?"

"I'm a Beamer!"

"Yes, Rollo told me…but I still don't know what a Beamer is!"

"Sorry, Faye, I keep forgetting how little you know about the land of Octavia. Right! Beamer Butterflies live on top of an enormous mountain. When we're very young we're taught to stare at the sun, for a short while to begin with, then for longer periods as we get older."

"But that's really bad for your eyes!" Faye was horrified!

"For your eyes, yes, and for the fairies, but in our case we store the warmth and brightness of the sun in our bodies, so that when we need to, we can shine beams of 'sunlight' from our eyes and see into the darkest of places. That's why we're the only creatures able to fly a human into these woods, because we can see!"

"Wow!" Faye was impressed. "So how…?" But at that moment, Brio spotted another swarm of Dots and off they went again.

They spent the next few hours following the same pattern. Brio would warn her to hold on, dive low or swoop high, and Faye would operate the box as he instructed. Sometimes they had as much as five minutes' rest before the next swarm, sometimes barely a second before Brio was off again.

It occurred to Faye that this was how Mr Tonal, the blind piano tuner, must feel. She remembered he had told her his hearing was better because he couldn't see, so she tried to really listen, and after a while she could hear the swarms of Dots swishing angrily a split second or so before Brio yelled, "Hold on!"

They made a great team, Faye decided, but she was more than a little relieved when Brio said wearily, "I think that's enough for now; we've captured far more than I expected on your first time out, well done!"

"Thanks, Brio. I tried my best."

"I know you did, Faye." Brio turned them around to face the opposite direction. "Back to the barn for the night."

"Oh good, I'm tired," Faye sighed.

"And then tomorrow, we'll start again!"

"Tomorrow? I thought we'd finished!"

"No, we've only just begun." Faye could hear the amusement in his voice.

"Right," she said quietly.

By the time they reached the barn, it was dark again and Faye was nearly asleep on Brio's back. She was vaguely aware of Rollo and a couple of others unclasping the riding straps and flying her down to a nice, warm, snuggly softness. She tried to say goodnight, but as soon as her head hit the pillow, Faye was fast asleep!

CHAPTER 11

"I think she should know EVERYTHING!" That was Forlana's voice, Faye decided, coming out of a deliciously deep sleep.

"I disagree." That was Rollo speaking quietly, Faye thought, so as not to wake her up. Faye kept her eyes closed.

"If you tell her about them, she may be too afraid to go out there again!" Rollo went on urgently. "She did so well yesterday. Let them go out today and see what happens. Even if they only catch as many as last night, that's still a massive amount!"

"It's not enough!" Forlana's angry voice took over again. "And what happens if she does run into them…and she's unprepared – tell me that?"

There was a hostile silence during which Faye decided she'd better pretend to wake up. So she turned over, did a lot of yawning and stretching, then opened her eyes.

"Hello, Faye, sleep alright?" Rollo came over with some milk and the little cakes every fairy seemed to eat.

"Yes, thank you," Faye replied, realising she was hungry.

"Viola will have your clothes ready in a minute."

Faye looked down and saw she was wearing a long, loose gown made of some soft, blue, fleecy material.

"She took your things to wash last night, while you were asleep."

"I must have been tired!" Faye was amazed; she hadn't even woken up during the process!

"You were exhausted – both of you." Rollo smiled kindly at her.

"Where's Brio?"

"He's resting too. Don't worry, he's fine. Just needed a good sleep, like you."

A plump fairy, dressed all in yellow, was coming across the barn bringing Faye's clean clothes with her.

"There's a little room over there where you can freshen up and change," said Viola, handing Faye her clothes.

"Thank you so much for washing them." Faye smiled shyly.

"No – thank you!" the fairy replied mysteriously, then went back the way she had come.

It didn't take Faye very long to get washed and dressed. There was even a sort of toothpaste and brush, although Faye didn't think the toothpaste was meant for humans; it made her teeth look pale blue in the mirror! She hoped they wouldn't always be that colour!

When Faye returned to the main room of the barn, she saw Forlana, sitting at a long wooden table, just finishing her breakfast.

Faye ran over to her and asked quickly, "Forlana, how's Landler?"

Forlana turned to look at her with a slight frown. "He's pretty much the same as yesterday; no worse, but he's no better either."

"I'm sorry," Faye said quietly, "I hoped he might have got better."

"Well, he hasn't!" Forlana snapped as she pushed herself away from the table and Faye, disappearing out of the barn door.

"She doesn't mean it, Faye, she's just upset." Brio had appeared behind her. She spun around to look at him and was shocked by what she saw. Where the camouflage paint had been evenly applied the day before, there were now great patches ripped off, showing Brio's lovely markings of red, orange and gold beneath, but in several places Faye could see bruises, scrapes and cuts. The only area that had escaped was where Faye's saddle had sat.

"Oh, Brio!" cried Faye in dismay. "What happened?"

"I'm okay, don't worry." Brio smiled. "You can't dive in and out of that forest without getting a few injuries!"

"But why haven't I got any, then?" reasoned Faye.

"That cloak you wore is stitched with magic to keep you safe. Humans are much more fragile than fairy folk...you have no magic to protect you!" He sighed.

"Well, it doesn't look as though yours has worked very well!" retorted Faye.

"Well enough." Brio laughed. "I'm still here!"

"But doesn't it hurt?" Faye looked at one or two of the worst hit areas and winced.

"I'm just about to be patched up now and then we'll be off."

Faye spotted two fairies approaching them, dressed in the same blue and white that the fairies who tended to Landler had worn. She supposed they must be some sort of medical fairies.

"I'll be back soon," promised Brio, as they ushered him into a large side room.

"Alright." Faye heaved a big sigh as she realised that today was going to be as great a challenge as yesterday had been...and that reminded her. She crossed to where Rollo was having his breakfast.

"Rollo, when I was waking up this morning you and Forlana were arguing about me…weren't you?" she added as Rollo looked about to deny it.

"Well," he replied thoughtfully, "not exactly arguing. It's just that everything's so difficult."

"Because Landler got hurt before he could teach me what I'm supposed to know?"

"Well…yes." Rollo looked up at her. "I wish I knew the best thing to do."

"I think the best thing to do is to tell me exactly what I need to know!" Faye sat down. "After all, I don't want to be 'unprepared', do I?"

"I was afraid you'd hear Forlana. That fairy couldn't speak quietly if she tried!"

Rollo sighed, then seemed to make up his mind. He turned to her with a serious expression and said, "Faye, I need you to listen to me carefully, for what I am about to tell you could save your life!"

Faye pulled her stool closer to the table and stared at Rollo so as not to miss a single word.

"The Dots that escape are drawn to the castle at the top of the highest hill."

"Dee Sharp's castle," murmured Faye.

"So you know about her?" Rollo was surprised.

"Yes. You told me, remember – the day that Landler got injured?"

"Ah yes, of course." Rollo sighed again. "Sorry, Faye, everything was a bit hectic that day."

"I know," Faye said sadly. "Sorry, Rollo, I interrupted you…you were saying?"

"Yes, well, Dee Sharp tries to entice every Dot to her castle and then, by her evil magic, turns them into…the Discords."

Although Faye had heard Forlana use the term before, it wasn't a word she was familiar with.

"What are they?"

"They're Dee Sharp's most powerful weapon," replied Rollo, solemnly. "They produce the Cacophony – a hideous, raucous noise, which, combined with her dark spells, will drive anyone mad who hears it."

"B…but won't WE hear it?" stammered Faye, really worried by this new threat.

"We hope not," Rollo tried to sound convincing…and failed. "You and Brio will both be fitted with special earpieces we've been working on, that will allow you to talk to each other, but, hopefully, should block out any other sounds…most of the time." He finished with a half-smile.

"A...and the r...rest of the time?"

"Well, a few years ago, we did have a few casualties. One child partly regained his hearing after three months...though he was never quite the same again. But the others..."

"The others?" repeated Faye.

"...we never saw them again."

"Oh..." Faye thought for a couple of minutes. She wanted nothing more than to go home right now and have a big cuddle with Mum, but then she pondered on what would happen to Cadence Falls if Dee Sharp won? How would merry Polka, quiet Rollo and Landler, who was still so ill, survive if the Discords managed to invade their peaceful little village?

She couldn't let that happen!

"I see," said Faye, looking straight at Rollo. "Thank you for telling me but, if Brio's willing, I still think we should go back."

"You're a brave girl, Faye, and we thank you, but I haven't told you the part that could save your life yet!"

"Yes, I would like to know that part." She smiled.

"Right! We've modified the Tremolo Vox Box with a special switch that you'll find just under the two buttons. If you get attacked by a couple of Discords, push the bottom of the switch in and it will magnify the vibrating note by a hundred."

"Wow!" Faye was impressed.

"This pure, constant note should literally pierce through the Discords and they'll disintegrate."

"Along with our eardrums!" Faye winced.

"No! You and Brio will be protected by your earpieces; all you will hear is a faint hum."

"Thank goodness!" Faye considered for a moment. "Rollo, you said a couple of Discords...what happens if there are more?"

Rollo looked down at his hands. "We can't be sure, Faye. You see, a Deluge happens so rarely; most of the time the Dots are all safely captured at the falls. But last time, two teams made it back, just, after a fight with three Discords. So, you see, we believe that if there are more than three..." he tailed off lamely.

"You don't come back," Faye finished for him. "I see. Any more tips you can give me?"

"Just don't EVER think about anything sad while you're in the woods. It's what Dee Sharp feeds on, and her magic will make the sadness in you grow and grow until you can't think and, more importantly, can't fight!"

"I know!" Faye suddenly realised. "I got sad thinking about Landler while we were in the woods yesterday and Brio had to shout at me to snap out of it!"

"Brio is the best we have." Rollo smiled. "You should be really safe with him."

As if by speaking his name they had conjured him up, Brio came in – his camouflage complete once more, but Faye could see lumps and bumps beneath the paint, where the dressings and bandages were. She crossed over to him.

"Brio, are you sure you're fit enough to go out again so soon?"

"I'm fine, Faye." Brio's words were meant to be reassuring, but Faye noticed the way he winced when he moved his left wing.

"You should both really have another bite to eat before you go out – you may not have the chance again today!" This was Viola, staggering under a heavy tray, laden with food.

Rollo dashed to help her and the two of them set it down carefully on the table.

Faye, munching on the delicious apple cookies, noticed that Brio only drank; first from a tall glass containing amber-coloured liquid, and then from a smaller, thin tube of glass where this time the liquid was the brightest red Faye had ever seen!

This made her a little nervous, especially as Brio kept glancing over his shoulder as if he didn't want this seen. (He needn't have worried as Rollo and Viola were deep in conversation!)

'I don't think butterflies drink blood,' she mused, 'but then Brio isn't an ordinary butterfly!'

However, she didn't have time to ask anyone about it, for no sooner had they finished their meal than everyone was rushing around them, getting them ready for their second foray into the Cacophony Woods.

After they were fitted with their earpieces and just as they were about to take flight, Rollo yelled something to Faye that she couldn't hear.

"Sorry, Rollo," she cried, lowering the hood of her cloak and removing the earpiece, "what was that?"

"I said, you're going further in, so the danger is greater! DON'T whatever you do TOUCH anything in the woods," shouted Rollo up to her, "or you'll never get out alive!"

CHAPTER 12

This time it seemed no sooner had they entered the woods than a swarm of Dots converged on them. At Brio's signal Faye swung the Vox Box around, pointed it at the largest group and pressed the silver button. Out sang the strong, trembling note she had heard the day before, and the Dots grew still. Entranced by the sound the group dived towards the nets. Quick as lightning, Faye pressed the gold button and the Dots disappeared.

Hours passed, with Brio and Faye repeating their joint manoeuvre over and over again, when all of a sudden Brio changed course and flew hard right.

"What's up?" asked Faye.

"I thought I saw…" Brio began, but then Faye saw too! Near a clump of ugly, brown trees were two large, oblong 'things'. (Faye couldn't think what to call them!) They were black and white and a few parts reminded Faye of something she'd seen before, but mostly the black and white had been muddled together, as if an artist painting a picture had angrily smeared it all with his hands. The result was a sticky, greyish-whitish mess, which made Faye feel rather sick.

"Discords!" yelled Brio. "Quick, the box!" Faye pressed the button; out sourced the note and then…the worst noise Faye had ever heard in her life blasted out all around them! It sounded like vacuums, blenders, trains, saws and the worst orchestra in the world were all playing at the same time! Even with her earpieces in the noise was immense!

"SWITCH!" yelled Brio.

Faye pushed the bottom of the switch in, as Rollo had instructed, and the vibrating note grew louder. Faye knew it was working as she could feel the note thrumming through her ribcage, but she couldn't hear it, thankfully.

The note grew still louder, but the Discords remained, fighting back with their hideous cacophony of sound.

"Hold on tight!" Faye wasn't sure if Brio was talking or if his voice was inside her head, but she could hear him. "I'm going around them; we'll try from a different angle!"

Brio zoomed off to the left and Faye flipped the switch again, but to no avail – the Discords were simply making too much noise, and the reason for this suddenly became dreadfully clear to Faye. Just above them a huge swarm of Dots was zipping about, but always heading in one direction – the castle on top of the hill!

"The Dots!" screamed Faye.

"I know," yelled back Brio. "The Discords are too powerful! The Dots can't hear the Vox Box because of the noise the Discords are making, so we can't capture them!"

"What can we do?" Faye couldn't bear to think they might fail in their mission, after all.

"I'm going higher to see if we can get beyond the range of those Discords, then we'll try the box again."

Beating his wings strongly, Brio rose higher and higher in pursuit of the Dots, until the air gradually became cleaner and they could see a little.

"Now, the box!" he yelled.

Faye pushed the silver button, and the note sounded, trembling clear and strong. The last of the swarm stopped to listen; Faye quickly pressed gold as they dived towards the nets… and they disappeared.

Brio flew on, trying to catch up with the rest. Faye was about to activate the box again, when a huge wave of the cacophony blasted out from the Discords, twice as loud as before!

Faye screamed.

"Reinforcements!" Brio cried, and sure enough, when Faye looked over her shoulder, she could see not two, not even three… but FIVE Discords rising up behind them!

'Five!' thought Faye. 'No one has ever come back after fighting FOUR!'

"Hang on!" At Brio's command, Faye clutched at the saddle as Brio began flying in a zigzag pattern, trying to lose the Discords. They thought they had succeeded for a while, as their pursuers dropped from sight, but then, just as Brio flew round a particularly nasty-looking tree, they saw only too clearly where the Discords had gone!

As Brio flew into the only open space Faye saw that the Discords had placed themselves like the four points of a compass so each way they looked, there was a Discord; and the fifth was hovering above them!

Brio quickly ducked among the branches of the tree.

"Faye," he said urgently, "I think they're planning to blast us from every direction; we won't survive that."

"I know." Faye shivered. "Brio, what can we do?"

Brio was silent for a moment.

"Faye, I need you to be braver than you've ever been before. Can you do that?"

"I… I don't know!" Faye was beginning to panic. "What… what do I have to do?"

"I need you to grip the saddle firmly with your left hand, undo the strap clips with your right, then slide off, still sitting on the saddle, and wait for me."

"But… WHERE?" Faye remembered Rollo's last words to her: 'Don't touch ANYTHING!'

Brio answered her carefully, "I am going to set you down… on a branch of this tree."

"WHAT?!"

"I don't have time to argue, Faye. It's this or we both die!"

With hands that trembled so badly she could barely get a grip, Faye carefully undid the clip that held the straps in place, then clutched the edge of the saddle so tightly that her knuckles showed white.

"Do it!" she said.

Brio gently manoeuvred as near to the biggest branch as he could manage.

"Right, slide down – it'll take your weight."

Faye slid down carefully, sitting on the saddle, feeding the straps through her fingers. Suddenly the whole thing came free, and with a dangerous wobble, she and the saddle dropped onto the branch.

"Right, Faye." Brio turned to face her. "I want you to sit cross-legged on the saddle, and don't touch anything else!"

Faye pulled her legs up carefully and crossed them.

"And Faye… I WILL come back for you!" He disappeared before Faye could reply.

She sat very still, holding tightly to the saddle on either side.

Then she saw Brio, who had taken up a position squarely in the middle of the Discords. Faye watched in horror, feeling certain this would be the last time she saw her friend, when… Brio burst into flames!

"No!" Faye screamed, as long tongues of red, orange and gold flame began to shoot out in all directions.

The Discords responded by trying to blast out the cacophony, but as they did so, the first Discord caught fire, crumbled, then disintegrated!

As Faye saw the second one start to burn, she cheered, but that made her overbalance. She reached out a hand to steady herself…

and touched the branch!

Suddenly all sounds ceased.

She was little again, maybe three or four, and was kneeling by her kitten, Snowy, who had just been run over. "Make him wake up, Mummy. Why won't he wake up?"

Faye began to cry, as other thoughts and visions invaded her mind. The day her favourite toy had got broken; all the times the kids had teased her at school because she couldn't swim. More and more – on and on – the sadness was relentless. It coursed through Faye until she was weighed down by grief and hopelessness.

"Fight it!" a faint voice inside her head… it was Landler's voice! Landler! Faye thought about the last time she had seen him: blasted by the Deluge, lying pale and unconscious. A great wave of despair hit Faye so hard that she cried out in pain, lost her grip on the saddle and began to fall…down…down…down.

CHAPTER 13

"Quickly! Give her the Sprite-Force Potion!"
"But – "
"Do it!"
The voice sounded oddly familiar but, somehow, miles away. Someone was trying to open her mouth. She was too tired to resist and opened it. Tingly drops of liquid went down the wrong way, making her cough.

'I think I'm in pain, but I'm not sure… my hand hurts, but…' The soft darkness reached out for her again…

"It's all my fault – I should never have made her go – I don't know if the Sprite-Force Potion is working! It's never been tried on a human before. Oh, why won't she wake up?"
The voice was strident, impatient and upset.

'It seems as though I have to wake up. Why is it so hard? Nothing's moving! I can't feel my feet or… wait a minute, something's happening!'

Very gradually a toe moved, then another. Finally the whole foot gave a twitch, then the other foot started, as if a wizard was casting a spell over her body, bit by bit.
Just as her knees woke up, the frantic voice said, "Look! She's beginning to move! Faye, Faye, wake up!"
"Shhh!" went a second, gentler voice.

'Faye… is THAT who I am?' The name danced around in her head for a few seconds. 'Faye… I'm Faye.' She tried it on for size. 'It sounds okay,' she thought, 'but who IS Faye? What does she do?'

As the potion worked its way up her body, she wriggled a bit more, testing her legs, then her fingers. When it got to her hands, there was pain in the left one; not too much, but enough to notice.

She reached out her arms, and the frantic voice said, "Cradle her head! Rollo! She'll come round in a minute!"

Rollo… did she know a Rollo? Strong arms went behind her head to her shoulders and gently moved her almost to a sitting position. Just as her shoulders were feeling a little less stiff, a bright light flashed inside her head, like a DVD player on fast-forward, images shot in front of her closed eyes, getting faster and faster. A waterfall – a green dress – fairies – Landler – Dots! – Pain! – camouflage – woods – Discords! – noise! – PAIN! – BRIO!!!

Faye woke up crying and screaming. She tried to fight off the arms that held her.

"Faye, Faye – listen, it's over. You're alright, you're alright!"

Faye found the strength to stop screaming, but she could not stop crying. Great shuddering sobs shook her whole body so badly she could hardly breathe.

She desperately wanted to shout out a name. Surely they must know the question she hardly dare ask?

"B…Br…Br…" she gasped.

"Brio is…" This voice was Rollo's, she decided, as it came from behind her, but it sounded so sad that Faye dreaded the next word.

"…alive." She took in a huge, sobbing breath and tried to open her eyes. She just managed a tiny glimpse (her eyes were red and swollen from crying too hard), but it was so blurred and watery that she quickly shut them again.

"Forlana, try giving Faye the Vivace Drops now, will you, please?" Forlana! That was it! Faye knew she recognised that voice! Forlana…Landler!

"L…L…Landler?" she managed to sob aloud.

"He's on the mend." Forlana couldn't disguise the relief in her voice. "It'll be a while before he's back to his normal, overbearing self, but he's out of danger."

"Good." Faye sighed, shakily. Why was she finding it so hard to talk?

"Here," Forlana said briskly, "open your mouth – I'm going to give you four Vivace Drops. I don't know if they'll work, but if they do, more than four might be dangerous."

Faye felt what tasted like little drops of her favourite lemon drizzle cake (but in liquid form) fall on her tongue and so she swallowed, carefully this time!

The effect was almost immediate: she stopped sobbing, shaking and shivering to begin with, then a lovely warm glow seemed to spread from her middle outwards.

This was all very well, but unfortunately, as her body began to awaken again, all the cuts, scrapes, bruises and blisters that she'd accumulated during her ride and the fall, all began to sting, ache, throb and smart all at once!

"Ow, ow!" Faye cried.

"It's okay, Faye. Believe it or not, it's a really good sign that you're hurting all over." Forlana sounded relieved.

"Well, it doesn't feel good to me!" snapped Faye, crossly.

"I know," soothed Rollo from behind her, "but it proves two things: one – that the Vivace Drops work on humans, and two – that you haven't done any lasting damage. We'd have been much more concerned if you couldn't feel anything!"

"Oh," said Faye, then changed it to "Ooh!" as a delicious coolness fell onto her closed eyes.

"I've just collected some dew," Forlana said. "Hopefully it'll reduce the swelling a bit."

"Thanks, Forlana." Faye felt something soft gently dabbing at her eyes to dry them.

"Try opening them now."

Faye slowly opened her eyes. They still stung a bit, but now she could see. To her surprise, she wasn't at the Red Barn as she had supposed, but lying on the grass, next to the Bar Barrier!

"Where are we?" she asked in alarm.

"Brio just managed to fly you to this side of the Barrier before he collapsed. He used the last of his beaming power to send up a distress beacon, which is how we were able to find you."

"Where IS Brio?" Faye swung her head round looking for her friend.

"Four of the other Beamers came and collected him because…he was too tired to fly himself."

"Yes, he must have been exhausted," Faye replied, but she couldn't help thinking that there was something else Rollo wasn't telling her. Then Faye noticed another thing – it was morning!

"How come it's morning?" she asked the fairies. "We left in the morning!"

"Yesterday," said Rollo, gently.

Faye turned to stare at him.

"Yesterday? We were gone all day and all night?" She thought hard…then she remembered the Discords' attack; Brio leaving her in relative safety on the tree branch…Brio going to fight them on his own!

"I must tell you," Faye began, starting to cry again.

"Not yet!" Forlana said sharply. "Now, Faye – we have to get you back to the barn. I need you to just concentrate on the here and now. We're going to fly you, just like Landler and I did that first day – do you remember?"

"Yes," Faye said, forcing herself to calm down.

"Good girl." Rollo moved from behind her and took her hands. "Try standing up… slowly."

Faye rolled sideways onto her knees then, letting Rollo take most of her weight, got to her feet, with several "Ooh"s, "Ow"s and "That hurt!"s along the way.

"Well done!" Rollo beckoned Forlana, who0 was gathering up her potions, to Faye's other side.

"We'll be as gentle as we can be, Faye, but it's probably going to be a bit uncomfortable for you. Fortunately we haven't too far to fly."

"Faye," this was Forlana trying, Faye realised, to sound kind and reassuring, "don't worry about anything. Just concentrate on flying with us and once we've got back to the barn, and you've had a bath and a hot meal, you can tell us about your adventure."

"Everything can wait till later," added Rollo.

"Okay." Faye smiled at the fairies and tried to look compliant, but she wasn't at all sure that what she had to tell them could, or should, wait till later!

CHAPTER 14

Rollo was right. It WAS an uncomfortable journey to the Red Barn. Faye could tell that the two fairies were doing their best not to jolt her about, for she saw them trying to synchronise their wingbeats so she wouldn't be pulled from side to side, but Rollo was a lot bigger and heavier than Forlana, so this wasn't entirely successful!

Faye gritted her teeth whenever a particularly sharp stab of pain occurred, and only allowed a small "Ow!" to escape her lips a couple of times. Before it became unbearable Faye saw, to her relief, the Red Barn down below them. The fairies descended gently and set Faye down, just before the barn doors.

"Take her in, Forlana," Rollo said, with a meaningful look, as he sped off in the opposite direction.

"Where's...?" began Faye.

"Bath and food first, remember?" said Forlana briskly, but not unkindly. She led Faye along, past the little bathroom she had used the day before, and then they turned into a much larger room.

"You go and soak in there and I'll find some food for you when you're finished."

"But where...?" Forlana had disappeared, leaving Faye talking to thin air, so she slowly opened the nearest door, which was shaped like half a church window, and went inside.

A wonderfully welcoming sight met her eyes. There were six massive, pale pink, spiral conch shells spaced out across the room. Scented steam rose from each of them and there were little matching curtains on runners to pull round each bath, hiding it from view. None of the baths were being used, Faye noticed. She chose the nearest one and pulled the curtain so that it formed a little circle round the bath, with just enough room to undress, and dry herself afterwards.

As she slipped off her clothes, (the earpiece and Vox Box must have been taken off while she was unconscious, she decided, for they weren't here now), Faye saw for the first time exactly how cut and bruised she was, and noticed the dark burn on her hand where she'd touched the tree. She nearly started crying again, but stopped herself by remembering that she'd need to tell the fairies exactly what had happened. She climbed up the three small steps carved into the lower side of the shell and then eased herself gently into the water. It was the most amazing bath she'd ever had!

At home, her mum was usually in a rush at bath time. "Come on, Faye, hurry up!" and she wasn't allowed to use Mum's Christmas bath stuff, so she'd never had the chance to just soak in a luxurious bubble bath! And that was another thing, Faye thought, as she tried to relax her sore and aching body in the water… bubbles in her world popped the moment you touch them, but these bubbles were like transparent ping-pong balls; they didn't pop – they just bounced around the bath!

Faye had huge fun bouncing them off the sides of the shell, and would quite happily have stayed in there for hours, if a hand hadn't suddenly appeared through the curtains.

"Ooh!" said Faye, startled.

"Sorry, Faye." It was Viola's voice. "I just came to bring you a gown and some towels. I'll pop them down here. Come out when you're ready. Forlana has food waiting for you."

"Thank you, Viola." Faye sighed. The way Viola had said that last sentence made Faye picture Forlana, waiting impatiently – tapping her foot! So Faye reluctantly climbed out of the bath and snuggled herself into the biggest towel to dry. She then slipped on another of the long, fleecy robes that she had woken up in the day before, only this one was lilac. She tried to wrap her wet hair up in the smaller towel, the way Mum did it for her, but she discovered this is much harder to do yourself, so she flipped her hair forwards and then back, so all the wet hair was off her face, and put the towel round her shoulders like a sort of cape, so her hair wouldn't soak the robe.

Back in the main room Faye found Forlana sitting at a table piled high with food.

She wasn't tapping her foot, but Faye thought Forlana might be tired of waiting for her, so she hurried across.

"Sorry, Forlana – I was a bit longer in the bath than I should have been."

"A bit?" started Forlana, then she looked up at Faye and they both laughed.

"Come and sit down, Faye. You need to eat plenty after your ordeal." Forlana sounded a lot less scary now, Faye thought.

"I'm sorry I've been so snappy with you, Faye," began Forlana, as Faye was served a huge amount of hot food by a plump fairy dressed in purple, "but what with Landler and then not knowing if you two were dead or alive, well…I don't do well under pressure!"

"It's okay." Faye smiled. "But please tell me now how Brio's doing?"

A tap on her shoulder from the chef fairy reminded her to keep eating, but she didn't take her eyes from Forlana's face, and saw the fairy's smile fade a little.

"PLEASE!" she begged, as she sensed Forlana was about to

reassure her. "Tell me how he really is!"

Forlana sighed. "He's so badly injured, Faye, that the truth is, we don't know! No Beamer Butterfly has ever done what Brio did last night... for all of us!"

"He...he just burst into flames," Faye whispered, reliving the moment again. "He shot them towards the Discords. I saw the first two go down, but then I think I fell..."

"That's what we can't understand, Faye – how come you weren't burnt when Brio activated the Blaze? Did your saddle strap break? We never found it."

"No...I wasn't riding on Brio when he did the...the Blaze thing."

"Not ON him?" Rollo had joined them quietly. "What do you mean, Faye, not on him – where were you?"

"Brio flew me to the biggest branch of the tallest tree, and made me slide down, still on the saddle, and sit cross-legged so I wouldn't touch anything."

"You got OFF?!" shouted Forlana, horrified.

Gasps went up from other fairies as they crowded round now, eager to hear what happened.

"Yes," said Faye quickly, "but Brio was right to make me; you know what happens when all those flames start shooting out – I'd never have survived!"

"We don't know, Faye," said Rollo in quiet amazement, "because we've never seen it happen. The Beamers have told us that in extreme emergencies they can blast out all their solar power at once, but no butterfly has ever done it, because without their power..."

"But Brio's still alive, Faye!" cut in Forlana quickly. "We don't know how, but he is!"

"You mean...he could die, because of me?!" Faye was aghast.

"Not because of you! You went out as a team, you both took the same risks!" cried Forlana, taking Faye's hand. "The most important thing now is that you tell us exactly what happened, right from the beginning. Don't leave anything out, however small it may seem."

"Okay." Faye took in a long, shaky breath, and started to tell the fairies about their second foray into the Cacophony Woods.

When Faye recalled exactly how many groups of Dots they had transported, some of the Music Fairies started making sounds of relief, but as soon as Faye mentioned their first sighting of the Discords, the room went completely silent as everyone stopped to listen.

After Faye had described the Discords in great detail, a few of the fairies made low moans, as if sick to their stomachs.

"...but the Discords were cleverer than us, they..."

"Wait a minute, Faye," interrupted Forlana, "what do you mean 'cleverer'? I've only ever seen one Discord and that was enough, believe me! But they have no intelligence whatsoever."

"That's what we thought, at first," agreed Faye, "but when the other three turned up we..."

"OTHER THREE?!" Rollo cried faintly. "How many did you have to deal with?"

"Five!" said Faye, impatiently. "Now, wait, let me go back a bit – I'm getting muddled with all these interruptions!"

"Sorry, Faye," said Rollo. "We'll try not to say anything else until you've finished."

"Thank you. Right! So we saw TWO Discords first. We sounded the

Tremolo note and then amplified it with the switch, but the Discords were making such an awful noise, that neither of us could hear our note at all!" Faye paused, as thirty fairies all gasped at once.

"Oh, that's right – you don't know, of course. The earpieces don't work; they might dim the cacophony sound a little, but they don't block it out."

Complete and utter dismay was plain to see on every fairy's face.

"How are you here? How did either of you survive?" whispered Forlana, her face pale.

"That was Brio," Faye went on. "He worked out that the Discords were blasting us with sound so that a particularly large swarm of Dots could escape. He flew higher and higher, so that we were out of range of the Discords, and we managed to capture some of the Dots, only about a third of the swarm – I'm really sorry we didn't get them all – but that's when the other three Discords turned up!"

Faye was concentrating so hard on remembering all of the details of the story that she didn't notice the looks of awe, respect and admiration she was getting from all the fairies.

"So, of course," Faye continued, "we couldn't do anything against five of them, and Brio tried flying zigzag to shake them off, but then suddenly, as we came round a tree, they were on all four sides of us, and one above, and…and then that's when Brio set me down on top of the saddle on a branch, and then…then he flew into the middle of them and started the Blaze. I saw him destroy two of them, but after that, I can't be sure! I think I must have touched the branch by accident, because then…" Faye shuddered as she recalled the terrible sadness that had taken hold of her. She swallowed. "I just kept thinking of all the horrible things that had happened to me and it got worse and worse…but then I thought I heard Landler's voice saying 'Fight it' and I really tried to…" Faye was crying now "…but thinking about Landler and how I'd last seen him was just too much, and I think I must have fallen."

There was complete silence as Faye came to the end of her story, broken only by the occasional soft sob from one of the fairies, every so often.

CHAPTER 15

Forlana took one look at her, gathered Faye up in her arms and gave her a huge hug, which surprised Faye so much that she stopped crying.

"Thank you, Faye – from all of us," said Rollo, rising to his feet. "The information you have just given us may well be what wins this fight at last!"

He called a few fairies, all of whom were dressed in brown, to him and said, "Right! The first thing we need to do is sort out those earpieces!" And off they all trooped to a room at the far end of the barn.

"Forlana," gasped Faye suddenly, "I forgot to tell them that the amplified note didn't disintegrate the Discords like it's supposed to!"

"It's alright." Forlana smiled. "I think they figured that bit out for themselves! Now, have some more to eat, while I tell you the part of the story you don't know!"

Faye reached for some berries from the nearest bowl and popped them into her mouth without even realising she was doing it.

"Brio," she said quietly.

"Yes." Forlana settled herself more comfortably on the bench. "We've only been able to get bits and pieces from the other Beamers, as Brio's been unconscious since we found him."

Faye winced, but didn't speak.

"Beamers communicate with each other in a different way to you and me. They send each other 'pictures' from one mind to another. Even though Brio isn't awake his brain is producing very clear pictures of three things. The first is seeing you fall and diving below to catch you, the second is looking back and seeing two Discords moving away from him, and the third is sending up his last ounce of power in the distress beacon. Apart from that, the Beamers couldn't find any more useful information, but he keeps flashing up one image over and over again."

"What is it?" whispered Faye.

"Your face." Forlana gently pressed Faye's hand. "You've made a good friend there."

"Yes – a good friend who nearly got himself killed, because of me!" Faye said bitterly.

"Don't you dare say that!" Forlana was angry now. "Brio knew the risks. This wasn't his first mission, after all! The human is always the most important factor because, although the Beamers can cross the Barrier, they can't work the Vox Box – you need a human to do that!"

"But…he blasted the Discords all by himself, while I was hiding in a tree!" she added, ashamed.

"Beamers are instructed to retreat if two or more Discords appear, because of what happened to the last three teams. However, Brio must have felt he couldn't get you back safely, because there were simply too many of them! He did the right thing – getting you out of the firing line while trying to take out as many Discords as possible." Forlana thought for a moment. "I've known a Beamer who ignited the Blaze to take out one Discord, when her human was injured by a falling branch, but she only used her front two jets for a few seconds before the Discord disintegrated. I've never known a Beamer use all their jets at once, as Brio must have done."

"I thought he'd burst into flames!" Faye recalled the panic she'd felt. "Why don't Beamers usually do that?" Faye had to ask, though she dreaded knowing the answer.

"Because," said Forlana gently, "Beamers live on the solar power they draw through their eyes when they are young. This is usually enough to last a lifetime, with an occasional top up during the height of summer, but if a Beamer uses every drop of solar power in their body then they usually…in most cases…"

"Die," Faye finished for her, numbly.

"Well, yes…but Brio's not dead," went on Forlana. "We're not sure what's keeping him alive, but something is!"

"For how long though?" Faye miserably reached for another handful of berries, this time from an orange bowl, without giving it much thought. She popped the berries into her mouth, bit into them, and at once felt as if her whole mouth was on fire. "Help!" she gasped as she choked, coughing and spluttering.

"What on earth…?" Forlana turned to face her, then saw the orange bowl.

"Oh my goodness! Faye, spit them out! I'm so sorry!" She reached round to slap Faye on the back. "How could I be so stupid? I brought in a bowl of glowberries instead of redcurrants! Quick! Someone get a dose of milkweed juice!"

A fairy in blue and white came running up with a small crystal container.

"Drink it, quickly!" cried Forlana.

Faye swallowed it in one gulp. It didn't taste very nice, but anything was better than the pain of her burning mouth! Gradually, the coughing and spluttering eased and Faye found she could open her streaming eyes once more.

A group of concerned fairies were all staring at her, and as if that wasn't bad enough, Faye saw she'd made a sticky mess on the floor where she'd spat the half-chewed berries out.

"I'm fine, I'm fine," she muttered, hoping they'd all go away so she could clean it up.

"Faye, I can't tell you how sorry I am…" began Forlana, but Faye, getting more embarrassed by the minute, slid down off her bench and began to clean up the mess with her towel.

"Leave that, we'll do it," said one of the medic fairies.

"No thanks, it's okay, I'm fine!" began Faye, when she looked at the bright blood-red of the chewed berries, and something suddenly clicked into place!

"Forlana," she said, getting up, "did you say these were glowberries?"

"Yes – they're meant for the Beamers. They eat them to supplement their solar power from time to time. They're not meant for fairies…or humans!" Forlana ended apologetically.

"How many do they usually eat at once?" Faye queried.

"Only two or three," Forlana replied. "They're really powerful. That's why I had to make sure you didn't swallow them!"

"But," Faye said slowly, trying to piece it all together, "suppose you crushed a load of glowberries and drank the juice…"

"What?" Forlana was alarmed.

"No… not me! Suppose Brio drank crushed glowberries and mixed it with something else. What would happen then?"

"He'd explode, I should think!" began Forlana, then she caught Faye's expression. "You don't mean that's what Brio did?"

"Just before we left, he drank a glass of amber liquid…"

"Nectar," Forlana nodded.

"…and then a glass of blood-red liquid," Faye finished.

Forlana's eyes grew round as saucers as she processed the new information.

"I think," she said slowly, "that though the glowberries would create extra flame power, the nectar would be sticky enough to retain some of it in the body…you know, like if you lit a fire, and then you let it almost die out, but not quite, so you could stoke it up again

later…Faye! You're a genius! I need to talk to the Beamers!"
Forlana rushed out of the barn to the infirmary before Faye could turn round!

'Some genius!' she thought. 'I nearly choked to death!'
But if her actions could save Brio, Faye decided she would gladly put up with a hundred burned mouths!

CHAPTER 16

Faye jumped up from the table and would have followed Forlana, had a wave of dizziness not suddenly hit her hard. She staggered back to the table and sat down again. What was wrong with her?

The crowd of fairies had now dispersed and there was no one left to ask, so Faye rubbed her forehead, glad to be on her own for five minutes.

As long as Forlana had come up with a plan to save Brio, Faye decided she couldn't summon the energy to think about anything else just yet.

She would have fallen asleep there and then, had a voice she knew only too well not said, "Hello, Faye."

She looked up, and there, in the doorway, leaning on a birchwood cane, was Landler.

"Landler!" screamed Faye, all tiredness and pain forgotten.

"Easy!" cried Landler as she went to fling herself at him. "I'm still a bit wobbly!"

"Of course, sorry." Faye hovered round him like an anxious hen over her chick as he limped across to the table and sat down.

"It's alright, Faye – I'm not that delicate, just have a bit more healing to do I guess."

Faye sat opposite him. "How did you get here?" she asked, indicating his stick.

"Brand flew me over. It was really hard to get it organised without Forlana finding out!"

"Who's...?" began Faye, then stopped as the impact of what Landler said hit home. "Forlana doesn't know you're here?"

Landler shook his head ruefully.

"I wouldn't want to be you when she finds out!"

Landler grinned. "The good thing is, now that I'm here she won't risk another journey sending me back."

"That won't stop her giving you a..." At that moment they both heard the shrill cry of, "Landler! Where? Wait till I get my hands on him!"

This was punctuated by small, running feet.

"Uh-oh." Landler braced himself for the onslaught as Forlana came round the barn door.

"Landler! Why are you here? You're supposed to be resting! How dare you…Wait a minute, how did you…?"

"Forlana," Landler caught hold of her agitated hands, "look at me, I'm fine!"

"Fine? Huh! I'll decide when you're fine! You could have set yourself back weeks, trying to do too much too soon!"

At those words, Faye broke in, "That's true, Landler, you're always saying 'not too much too soon'!"

"Hey, whose side are you on?" Landler smiled, but Faye's words diffused the situation and Forlana sighed, then clipped her brother gently round the ear.

"Well, there's one good thing. While you're here you can be looked at in the infirmary – no arguments!" she added as she saw Landler about to protest.

"Agreed." Landler sighed.

"Right!" Forlana sat down next to Faye. "I told the Beamer Healer what you told me and he thinks, with the right infusion of nectar and glowberries, Brio should pull through."

"That's wonderful!" cried Faye, relieved. "When can I see him?"

"Not yet. There's a long way to go still."

Forlana tried to sound reassuring, but the worry came through in her voice.

Landler looked at Faye. "Brand told me a little of what happened, but I don't know the whole story. I think he got some bits wrong anyway, because he said you fell from a tree, and that can't be true!"

Forlana and Faye glanced at each other. Faye was very relieved when Forlana said, "I'll tell him, shall I, Faye? Save you going through it again."

Faye nodded and sat quietly while Forlana gave Landler all the facts of both journeys Faye and Brio had taken into the Cacophony Woods.

When Forlana reached the part where the amplified Tremolo Note had failed to disintegrate the Discords, Landler's expression became serious and stern, and then, as Faye knew he would, he jumped up, forgetting his pain when Forlana reluctantly told him that Brio had set Faye down on the branch.

"He did WHAT? I'll have his hide for this! How dare he!"

"Landler!" Both girls stood as one to push him back down on his seat.

Faye was angry. "If Brio hadn't done that we'd both be dead by now – do you understand? He had to do it… he saved my life!" She sat down, choking back the tears that threatened to fall again.

"But…but…" Landler couldn't get his head round it. "It goes against everything we know about the forest. The first rule has always been – TOUCH NOTHING!"

"I agree," said Faye, "and if I'd sat on the branch I probably wouldn't have survived."

Landler nodded.

"But I didn't," Faye went on. "I sat on the saddle on the branch, and if I hadn't slipped and touched the branch accidentally…" here she turned over her left hand so Landler could see the three small burns where her skin had touched the bark "…I'd have been fine. All the other cuts and bruises I've got were caused by the fall, same as if I'd fallen from an ordinary tree at home." (Although this tree was about four times taller than any tree she'd seen in the park, Faye thought, but she wasn't about to tell Landler that!)

Landler looked again at Faye's burnt hand, then held it very carefully. "We asked too much of you, Faye," he said quietly. "If I hadn't been injured, I would never have let you do this. Forlana," here he looked at his sister, "how could you?"

"She had no choice!" broke in Faye before Forlana could reply. "She had to tell me about the Discords and Dee Sharp to save Cadence Falls and all the fairies, and once I knew I was the only one who could cross the Barrier on Brio, well…I had to go, didn't I?"

"But you're so young and…and human!" whispered Landler, troubled.

"I can't help being young." Faye smiled. "And if I wasn't human, well…" She spread her hands to make her point.

"I know, I know, you had to go…but Faye, you do realise that the sadness and anger that entered you when you touched the tree will try to weaken you every time you're in the forest?"

"I thought it might," Faye answered him. "Even here, when I was telling everyone what happened, I felt this huge sadness – it was so heavy!"

"That's it! You must always be on your guard against it, Faye. It could creep up on you at any time."

"Don't worry, Landler. Now that I've seen you, as soon as I know Brio's going to be okay, I'll have nothing to be sad about!"

"I'll go check in on him, Faye, if you'll make sure this idiot doesn't go anywhere!" Forlana rose as she spoke, casting a mock-glance at Landler as she left.

"She was so worried about you, Landler," Faye told him. "I don't know how she kept everything going here, when all she wanted to do was be with you."

"Forlana's a born organiser." Landler smiled. "She knew she'd be much more useful here – she makes a terrible nurse!" He laughed. "She's too impatient and wants everything to happen at once! I'd have probably had a relapse if she'd been looking after me!" Faye laughed with him.

"Don't let her know," Landler added, "but one of the fairies told me she flew back every night to check on me. Forlana would hate it if she thought I knew she cared; she thinks emotion is a sign of weakness."

"That's why she ran off every time she cried. She didn't want any of us to see!" Faye realised. It explained why Forlana had been so angry; she thought anger was better than tears.

"Forlana, crying?" Landler was astonished. "About what?"

"You – of course!" Faye burst out laughing at the look on his face. He smiled back and then quickly changed the subject as Forlana came back.

"Yes…so Brand's a Beamer just like Brio. I've known him all my life and persuaded him to fly me in so I didn't miss all the fun."

"I'll be having words with him later!" Forlana chided as she overheard the last part of their conversation. "I've been wondering how you managed to get here!"

"Forlana," Faye cut in, "how's Brio doing?"

"Better now. They've started the infusion and it's boosting the power he managed to retain. They say they think he's going to be fine."

"Yes!" Faye did a little clap of excitement, just as Rollo came over to their table.

"Landler! Good to see you. How are you feeling?" Rollo greeted him.

"Not too bad, just a bit banged up." Landler rubbed his wrists ruefully where Rollo had grasped it.

"Oops! Sorry!" Rollo turned quickly to Faye. "We've made a few modifications to those earpieces. Would you mind coming to try them out?"

"Of course." Faye started to rise from the table when Landler put a hand out to stop her.

"No. Sorry, Rollo. I know it's important, but Faye needs rest. She has to go home."

"But I thought Forlana wanted you to stay here now," began Faye, but Landler shook his head.

"Not to my home, Faye, I meant back to your home."

Faye stared at the fairies. "But…but you can't make me leave now! We need to go back in – there are still loads of Dots loose in there. Maybe your friend Brand could fly me until Brio's better…"

"I told you she was special," Landler said to Forlana, who nodded in agreement.

"Faye, you've already done so much for us, more than any other human has since…since Greenbow!"

"Who's Greenbow?"

"A story for another time," Forlana broke in. "The point is, Faye, humans can only survive for a little bit at a time in our world. They need to go back to theirs to grow, be nourished and to do all the things that make them human!"

"But I will be able to come back again?" pleaded Faye.

"I'd like to say no – you've done enough," said Landler, seriously. "But the fact is, we need you! You've only been here a few days, yet in that time we've learned more about the Dots, the Discords and the forest than we ever knew before. I have a feeling we'll be seeing a lot more of you."

"Hurray!" Now that Faye knew this, she felt a lot happier about leaving. "There's just one thing first. Forlana…"

"I know, I know." Forlana turned to leave. "I'll go and ask if you can see Brio, and also," with another glare at Landler, "see if your 'pet' will give us a lift to the Mezzo Meadow!"

"He will!" Landler called after her.

"Now, Faye, before I forget, you must take this." He took a long, thin, roll out of his cloak.

"What is it?" Faye asked as she took it.

"A Sotto Voce Practice Mat. Remember when you asked how you were supposed to actually practice when your mum would think you'd already done an hour?"

"That seems like ages ago!" Faye gasped.

"I know," agreed Landler, "but we have to make sure everything is in place now. If you unroll it you'll see every note that's on your piano at home is here, too. The difference is, when you practice on this, no one will hear the notes, except you!"

"I can practice in my room," Faye smiled. "And mum will never know."

"You must be careful though, Faye. This mat is made of a special weave that can exist in your world, as well as ours. It won't do to let anyone find it."

"I know!" Faye cried. "I've got an old shoebox in my wardrobe. It's got stuff in from when I was a baby – Mum never looks in it now!"

"Perfect." Landler smiled. "Here comes Forlana, and from the look of her I should say she's bullied the Beamers into letting you see Brio…and she's got you a lift back!"

CHAPTER 17

Flying on Brand was similar, but somehow different to flying on Brio, Faye decided. She supposed it was because she and Brio seemed to have a special connection, even before their battle with the Discords.

She'd seen Brio, briefly. The Beamer medics who were caring for him told her he'd woken up once and asked for her, but before they could send word, he'd become unconscious again.

"We told him you were safe and not too badly hurt, and that seemed to relieve his mind, so it's best he just sleeps for now," one of the medics told her. "You can go in and see him, only for a minute, though, and don't worry about how he looks – it's all there to help him."

Faye had tiptoed cautiously in and then stopped as she took in everything that surrounded Brio. Amidst a lot of tubes, containers and syringes he was lying face down on a large pallet. His wings - his whole body, in fact - was wrapped in something that looked a bit thicker than a cobweb, pale green in colour and, when Faye put out a finger to touch it, very soft.

She could see Brio's face, at least part of it. The right side was bandaged, including his eye, and Faye turned to the medic, the question written all over her face.

"Before you ask, we don't know if we can save his eye," he said, sadly. "I'm afraid it's just a case of wait and see."

"He must get well, he must! He saved me!" whispered Faye, stroking the bandages gently.

"We've started him on the infusion of nectar and glowberries, thanks to you, and it seems to be…" At this moment the Medic Beamer paused and stared into space. Faye knew enough to realise he was probably communicating with another Beamer, so she waited.

"Brio knows you're here." The medic smiled. "He sent me a picture of you riding on his back, laughing, and the picture is edged in blues and lavenders which, in our language, mean love and happiness."

"Oh, Brio!" cried Faye. "I'm so glad you know I'm here. I have to go back to my world now, Landler says, but I'll be back, I promise!"

"I'll tell him." The Medic Beamer ushered her out. "He's too exhausted to hear you now."

And that had been the end of her visit.
Faye sighed.

"Are you alright, Faye?" Forlana couldn't swivel round to see Faye perched up behind her, but she'd demanded (and got) two sets of the earpieces Faye had worn, so they could talk on the flight.

"Just worried about Brio," Faye replied.

"Don't be." Forlana sounded positive. "I've known Brio for a very long time and he's just about the bravest, toughest Beamer there is. He'll pull through!"

"I hope you're right, Forlana."

"Of course I'm right! Now listen, Faye, there isn't much time. Once we arrive at the Mezzo Meadow, I will activate the Rubato charm – you will look through your Clef Crystal, follow the Sparkle Path and return to your piano. Exactly five seconds after that, your mum will come in from the kitchen with milk and a biscuit."

"How on earth do you know that?" Faye was puzzled.

"Because 'Rubato' means robbed time. We have 'robbed' three days' worth of time from your world and given it to you here, in ours, but in order for it to work, we have to put a few spells in place, like making sure your mum doesn't come in while you're away, and making sure we know what will happen for at least five seconds after you return."

"Where do you rob the time from?" Faye was intrigued.

"From all the humans who waste it," Forlana replied, sadly. "There are some people who say, 'I can't be bothered' or 'I'll do that tomorrow' and then never do. All of that wasted time has to go somewhere, so we fairies use it and make the most of the time – do you understand?"

"I think so," Faye mused, "but I'm not going to waste any time!"

"Glad to hear it," was the rejoinder. "We have far too much to do!"

Just as the Mezzo Meadow came into view Faye remembered something she'd meant to ask before. "Forlana, when I thought I was going to die in the forest when I was so sad, I heard Landler's voice in my head saying, 'Fight it!'. How come?"

"Of course you did!" Forlana sounded surprised she'd needed to ask. "Landler is your Mentor. Even though he got injured before he could start teaching you properly, he'd still made the link with you."

Faye was confused. "What's a Mentor?"

"Someone who is older and wiser than you, who acts as a combination of teacher, advisor and role model."

"Oh, I see…and the link?"

"The link is the bond that the fairies make with the humans they are training. It enables him to 'link' with your thoughts in an emergency."

"Will I be able to hear Landler in my world?"

"I shouldn't think so." Forlana was doubtful. "There's a big divide between the fairy and human worlds. It's never been tried before."

"Oh, I see." Faye thought for a moment then said, with a note of rising anxiety in her voice, "But how will I know when you need me to come back? You might be in real danger and I wouldn't know!"

"Now, don't panic!" Forlana told her with mock severity. "That's what your Clef Crystal is for: if we need you, we'll activate the Aria Stone to the pitch of your crystal, which will cause you to play the sequence of notes that opens the portal."

"Wow!" Faye was impressed.

"Now, Faye," Forlana said just as they were about to land in the Mezzo Meadow, "don't expect to come back straight away. You need at least two- or three – weeks' recovery time in your own world before you can return to ours – maybe longer."

"But…please!" Faye begged.

"You're no use to us if you're not properly healed," Forlana told her bluntly. "We need you to be at maximum strength if you're going to help us defeat Dee Sharp!"

"Well, I am going to; there's no doubt about that!" was Faye's determined reply.

"Good, now, get ready to dismount as soon as Brand lands."

Faye did so easily. She'd practised with Brio, after all. She thanked Brand as he flew to a large clump of lilac flowers and had a long drink of nectar and dew.

Forlana turned Faye to face her. "Now, Faye, before you leave, a few words of advice which Landler would have given you if he'd been here. First of all – PRACTISE! I know you find it boring but practising on your piano is just about the most important thing you can do for us Music Fairies in your world. We need you to be able to play well and understand more about how music works, because then, each time you come back to us, your music will make you stronger."

"I will," promised Faye.

"Secondly, let no one see your Practice Mat. It's too unusual to have come from your world, and people will start to ask questions."

"Okay. I told Landler where I could hide it."

"Good girl...and finally, and this is, perhaps, the hardest thing of all: you cannot tell anyone about your adventures here, not even your mum!"

"But...why not?" Faye queried.

"For one thing, grown-ups wouldn't believe you, and if your friends found out, they'd all be trying to get here and that would be a disaster. We only let a few human children in and they have to be very special."

"But I'm not..."

"Don't ever say that again!" Forlana snapped. "You've done more to save us than almost any other human I've known! You ARE special, Faye – believe it!"

Faye sighed. "Okay, Forlana, if you say so."

"I do." Forlana smiled as she took from her pouch a small red disc. "Now we just need to return you to human size again."

"Human size?" Faye was confused.

"Of course! You didn't think you could sleep in a walnut shell and bathe in a conch without being fairy size, did you? You wouldn't fit!"

"I did wonder about that," Faye said.

"As you return to your world, you'll also return to your correct size." Forlana moved a small section of the red disc to the right and placed it on the grass in front of them and...nothing happened.

"Oh! What's gone wrong?" cried Faye.

"You have!" Forlana laughed. "You forgot to look through your Clef Crystal!"

"Oh yes, of course!" Faye raised her crystal on its chain in front of her eyes. There was the blue and silver archway she'd last seen in her lounge, and the path of sparkles leading to it.

"Goodbye, Faye," called Forlana, as Faye took her first step onto the Sparkle Path. "Remember, time doesn't always go at the same pace in each of our worlds, so you may come back what's tomorrow for us, or it may be months later!"

"Okay, Forlana. Bye!"

Faye took the final step through the arch and was, once more, back in her own lounge, in her own house, in her own world.

CHAPTER 18

Faye just had time to slip onto the piano stool before Mum came in.

"Well, Faye, that's got to be the longest practice session you've done yet!"

"Is it? I hadn't really noticed the time," said Faye innocently, taking the glass of milk and a biscuit her mum had brought in. Forlana had been right about that!

"You can watch an hour of TV before dinner if you'd like, as a reward." Mum smiled.

Faye was just about to say, 'Yes please,' when she remembered that now she had to actually go and practice on her Sotto Voce Mat!

"Thanks, Mum" she said, "but I've got some reading to do before dinner, in my room, if that's okay?"

"Of course," replied Mum. "I'd much rather you weren't wasting time watching TV!"

Wasting time? Faye took a deep breath.

"Mum, you know how you wanted me to have swimming lessons?"

"Yes," sighed Mum. "I was sorry you said you didn't want to learn; swimming is such good fun."

"Well." Faye smiled. "I've changed my mind. Please could I have them now?"

"Yes, of course! Aunt Laura was very keen for you to learn. What's happened to make you have a change of heart?"

Faye grinned. "It's just that I'd like to go swimming with a couple of friends of mine sometimes."

"I'll ring Aunt Laura right now and see if it's still alright to book them – I'm sure it will be."

Mum was gone in a flash.

Faye collected her music book from the piano, and as she went up to her room she thought, 'Well, I certainly won't be wasting my time! I've now got extra piano practice, schoolwork, visiting Great Aunt

Laura AND swimming lessons to fill up my time.'

Once in her bedroom, Faye carefully unwrapped her Sotto Voce Mat that she'd kept safely hidden underneath her T-shirt, opened the book Miss Hummingstone had given her, and took a deep breath.

If the Music Fairies needed her to practice, then practice she would!

She touched the middle C on the mat: a soft, mellow little note sounded, like a fairy's hum, just for her ears alone.

'Right,' thought Faye, 'here we go, then…'

Twinkle… Twinkle…

ABOUT THE AUTHOR

Paul Govier-Simpson was born in 1951 in Beckenham, Kent, and considered herself a true Kentish maid.
Growing up as an only child, with health complications at an early age, she learnt to delve into her over-active imagination, creating plays and elaborate stories for her dolls whilst she recuperated from Asthma and Pneumonia.
She learnt to sing from her Aunt Mabel who was a concert hall pianist, and from her father who was a big hit in the early music hall days, and would often be found singing in harmony with them around the piano at Christmas.

Paul also had a big passion for Ballet, going on to study at the Royal Academy of Dance and joining the Scottish National Ballet, where she enjoyed many years touring with them.
When her dance career came to an end, it was time to find a new passion that she could really sink her teeth into, and so she began choreographing for local Amateur Dramatic Societies, and then later directing musicals.
During this time, she also wrote several of her own musicals and plays, including her favorite "The Rainbow Bird" in the early 80's.
She then went on to run various children's drama groups, and created her very own choir "Giocosa Cantabile" where at one stage, there were 20 students all singing in 4-part harmony, winning several awards at various music festivals.

When Paul and her husband decided to move to Devon in 2015 to be closer to their daughters and grandchildren, she got the idea to write a series of books combining two of her favorite things, music and fairies, and thus "Faye & the Music Fairies" was born.

This is Paul's first ever publication, and will sadly be her last, after her passing from a terminal lung disease that took her on the 1st of February 2020.
Her youngest Daughter was left the books, and given the task to get them published for the world to read, and so in Paul's honor she has done just that.
"Faye & the Music Fairies – The Clef Crystal" is the first book in a set of 6 stories that will be published.

Printed in Great Britain
by Amazon